REEL

By Laurence M. Janifer

REEL

KNAVE IN HAND

SURVIVOR

POWER

THE WAGERED WORLD
(with S. J. Treibich)

THE HIGH HEX
(with S. J. Treibich)

TARGET: TERRA
(with S. J. Treibich)

A PIECE OF MARTIN CANN

IMPOSSIBLE?

YOU SANE MEN

THE WONDER WAR

SLAVE PLANET

BRAIN TWISTER
(with Randall Garrett; as "Mark Phillips")

THE IMPOSSIBLES
(with Randall Garrett; as "Mark Phillips")

SUPERMIND
(with Randall Garrett; as "Mark Phillips")

MASTERS' CHOICE
(editor)

REEL

LAURENCE M. JANIFER

DOUBLEDAY & COMPANY, INC.
GARDEN CITY, NEW YORK
1983

Library of Congress Cataloging in Publication Data
Janifer, Laurence M.
Reel.
(Doubleday science fiction)
I. Title. II. Series.
PS3560.A52R4 1983 813'.54

First Edition

Library of Congress Catalog Card Number 82–45293
ISBN: 0-385-17757-7

Printed in the United States of America

For Seligmann, Shaw & Kidd,
Keepers of the Faith:
and very particularly for
Fred Phillips:
friend, gadfly, poet.

REEL

FIRST CALL

CHAPTER 1

Suppose then there were a man so clever that he could take all kinds of shapes and imitate anything and everything, and suppose he should come to our city with his poems to give a display, what then? We should prostrate ourselves before him as one sacred and wonderful and delightful, but we should say that we cannot admit such a man into our city; the law forbids, and there is no place for him. We should anoint his head and wreathe about it a chaplet of wool, and let him go in peace to another city, but ourselves we should employ the more austere and less pleasing poet and storyteller, for our benefit. He should imitate for us the speech of the good, and should tell his tales on those patterns for which we made our laws at the beginning, when we were trying to educate the soldiers.

—from *The Republic,* Book III, by Plato,
translated by W. H. D. Rouse

ALEX YONGE

CHAPTER 2

It's quite possible, when I take time to think of it, that this story is being told by the wrong person. In fact, I'd be perfectly willing to bet (and, naturally, I'm not much of a betting man) that I'm as wrong a person for the job as any you might be able to think of; but, then, the Undersecretary (who wants all of what happened set down for the record, for, as you may believe, some official statement or other) happened to choose me—and that, after all, is quite finally and entirely that. I should imagine that he picked my name, simply, out of a hat, or found himself involved in some other method of choice that had nothing truly to do with me, with my actual person; but that's none of my business here, and I don't suppose (whoever you are, and whatever, finally, these records are for) that it can be any business of yours, either. But, you see, we don't argue with the Comity anymore. None of us do, out here, since in the end argument pays for nothing; besides, we're out of practice, not having had any government to speak of for so long a time. You must understand that we're no sort of anarchist-world, nothing in the least of that type; but what we have here can't quite be described as a government, either, and, when there are other, true, governments with which to deal, we're put a little at a loss. For the most part there are none, and so, left to ourselves, we take the easier road and deal only with people, with, in fact, individual wants and needs, drives and ideas. And now—look for yourselves—I'm afraid that, in spite of all my good resolutions and all my various training, I've begun somewhere near the middle of all this, and succeeded only in making a new confusion; this is hardly the way, after all, to begin what should have been a controlled and a complete report.

On the other hand, if the Undersecretary (oh, we're patriotic enough, I suppose; at least, we call things by their right names)—if he wanted that sort of thing, he should have picked a political commentator, or whatever one of those people might be called; and, for all I know, when I consider the matter, it's perfectly possible that he did. Except, of course, that political commentators are another sort of thing we're not truly familiar with, here on Three.

To be frank, this is all one confusion right now, mostly, I imagine, because I have no clear idea of my starting-point, and I'm only passing time talking this into the machine, without enough thought; well, I'm young, as you may have guessed, and the habit of true thought and true care takes a long while to develop. At twenty-two, I can give an order with as much authority as the next man, but no one finally expects me to consider every possibility, not for another ten years, or perhaps twelve. There is a rule for this report, as it was explained to me: start anywhere (and I assume the same rule was given to the others when they began, if in fact there are any such "others." One of the peculiarities of this particular job is that I simply do not know who else has been asked for a report, or whether anyone else at all is involved in the record with me. I don't even know finally what this report is for, though that, as I've said, is none of my affair; there is a somewhat strongly worded request for secrecy, too, which would make matters difficult and risky; only, in fact, foolishness would dictate a decision to discover who else is involved with me here). Not that all my parenthesis makes any true difference: the rule is the same in any case, and the rule requires me to start. Which, as you will notice, I'm not yet doing; the Undersecretary and the Comity, I'm afraid, will just have to put up with me.

(If, by the way, I make an occasional joke, don't mind it; I do such things only to relieve pressure; fundamentally, in fact, I'm quite a serious chap.)

Perhaps the place to start is with the fight. And yet . . . in order to explain the fight I ought, quite possibly, to search further back among the days; and then, in order simply to explain the explanation, I should be forced to begin finally with the original founding of Three. (Which, of course, I'm calling by its official name, its truly proper name; the usual practice is to call it the Reel, and you may be more familiar with us under that label. I don't know how our nickname began; we're called Three, of course, because we're the third planet out from our star, quite like old original Earth, where everything and all began, even the Comity of Planets and such beings as Undersecretaries; but why we're called the Reel I truly couldn't say.)

I can't keep on traveling backward forever, though; so here, at last, is the fight, and my own true beginning.

I think Frain was on edge, and trying to get a rise out of me, as we say, but naturally I couldn't stand still and be told, quite flatly, that our gaffs were squat—our hidden tricks too ancient; it isn't the sort of statement one can take with a smile and a brush-off, and it didn't seem to matter much to me where we were, or when; so I hit him, and he went flying off more or less on one leg with his arms out and pinwheeling, making a few unpleasant sounds while the customers just stopped everything to watch, wondering, perhaps, if this youngster in the blue skintights had been caught cheating or had possibly caught the management cheating him, or, at any rate, something dramatic of that sort. The main gaming room might have seemed no place for a fight, and my father would have "objected with guns," as the phrase is, but you take an opportunity where it waits for you—and, anyhow, I feel the tourists truly expect some sort of brutal action every few spins; then they feel more like outlaws. The feeling must be kept alive that Three is a dangerous place; they accept the place more happily if they think that.

No one, at any rate, left; they all stood, quiet and still, watching me and watching Frain as he began to recover. That main gaming room of ours is a true palace of a place, big and shining quite the way it ought to be, with a ceiling fifty feet high, vaulted and covered over with gold and glitter, mirrors everywhere (all, of course, tinted so that you look healthy and happy no matter how much you may have lost; such trade secrets don't matter, the effect being quite the same if you know, or you don't know, the mechanism used to produce it), our girls circulating through the tourists' gatherings with drinks and sandwiches, every last hostess in the latest, the brightest, the most pleasing of the cutaway fashions and every one guaranteed by our makeup crew to look sympathetic, willing and under twenty-five, eight hours in every day, five days in every week. Three, naturally enough, is an extremely personal-service world, and the look of our hostesses made our prices worth anybody's while; though, of course, the hostesses were, on shift, only for show. Their offtime's their own, and what do we care?—but inside the rooms they rest strictly on business, under threat of real trouble, possibly even an assignment to one of Marge Sunday's specialty groups, with not a chance on Three to duck away or find themselves excuse or out. So: there, inside the Palace, the tourists were circulating and chattering and gaming away, betting, copping or ducking while the stickmen kept the action constant, never pressing, always moving, the whole room like one single smoothly operating machine, the tourists going in one end, the money coming out the other, keeping every last single person on and off the world, all at the same time, satisfied, relaxed, in fact happy. The overhead on a place like that is fantastic (no other word, I'm afraid, will do), but we can afford it: every tourist simply has to imagine that he's the one to break us—or else, more simply, he's a "compulsive gambler," if the phrase is more than a sound-series for you; it might, in fact, truly mean something after all. There was once a tourist here who claimed to be a psychologist, or some such sort of thing, one I met at a reasonably quiet part of Marge Sunday's; he didn't find himself attracted at all by our sort of flash, but, he told me, he was familiar enough with people who did, and he explained to me just what made them operate; the explanation was, simply, a string of such words and sounds. I only wonder, now and again, what made *him* operate; after all, he was here, too, wasn't he?

I do go on, as you'll notice, interrupting myself; perhaps this will be an easier job as it goes on. At any rate, to return: I slammed Frain and he went skidding, and all that lovely action in the gaming room stopped while heads turned to watch us. I did no more than stand and wait for him to recover, not following up my advantage because this was more or less a friendly battle, and Frain hit a set of roulette lights and balanced himself and came back swinging. The tourists opened a big aisle for him and I was at the end of it. His fist hit me on the side of the cheek and the rock he wore on one finger left a mark that was set to turn to bruise, but I was fading to the side and he didn't cut me: made me mad all over again, that was all, and my ears ringing. So, I continued that duck-away, let one of his ham hands go over my head and butted him under the left ribs, hard enough to knock out of him a little wind. I heard him whoosh out with that, and came up with a balled fist I aimed mostly by sound, as well as I recall, and I connected: he went over backward and lay on the rug. We have an expensive rug, which isn't important, and it looks expensive as well, which is. (If I'm not careful I'll end this by writing a textbook covering our life on Three, and I truly wouldn't want many tourists to read such a record as that.)

We have a contract arranged with a decent corps of bodyguards, naturally enough, and they were already lifting Frain off the rug, and the stickmen were calling the action, the crowd melting away, though a few of them went on staring at me, all dressed as I was in the livery of the house; and in the fading of confusion I heard a few tourists wondering who I was, though only one of them made the right guess and called me the eldest son: other worlds don't appear to think in the same sort of patterns we do here, and the idea of an eldest son being important doesn't truly occur to them very often.

I took their stares without thinking too much about them, being at the moment more occupied with what I was going to tell my father, and I had even a little attention to spare for Frain, who was beginning to come out of the fog as the guards set him on his feet and started him through the room. He blinked a couple of times, and looked as if he wanted to form words, but I became for some reason polite, and spoke first.

"Good fight, Frain."

He licked his lips and asked, "Was it?" His voice was a little indistinct, and he had some trouble keeping himself under true control.

"Friends?"

He grinned at me, giving me an expression I somehow found myself mistrusting. "You'll find out," he told me in a voice both low and harsh. "There's a little surprise waiting for you one of these days." It took him some time to produce so many words as that.

"We'll meet again," I told him. "Whenever you say." I thought, of course, that he was setting himself to frame a new challenge, which would have been the common, almost, perhaps, the expected thing.

"It's not that sort of surprise," he said.

The words puzzled me, even then, and, perhaps, shook me a little; so I imagine you might call that moment our beginning. And if my squaring-away there in the gaming room had in fact been my mistake, then Frain had evened matters by making one of his own; and that, too, helps in finding the true beginning, the first moment of the record.

It all, in fact, seems very small; but bigger matters have started with smaller events, I imagine; and, at any rate, the fight was the first true event that I was able myself to experience, and I'm the one set to talk this out and down: to that extent, at the very least, the record is mine.

So, whether, unimportantly, I knew the fact or not, we were off and running. And for all I know to the contrary, it's quite possible someone was making book on me.

If so, I hope I was marked for good odds.

SECOND CALL

CHAPTER 3

They dance around the dying, & they drink the howl & groan
They catch the shrieks in cups of gold, they hand them
to one another:
These are the sports of love, & these the sweet delights of
amorous play
Tears of the grape, the death sweat of the cluster the last sigh
Of the mild youth who listens to the lureing songs of Luvah

—from "Milton," by William Blake

MARGARET SUNDAY

CHAPTER 4

There seems to be a troublemaker in every batch, and the first duty I have is to find her—a duty, I suppose, to myself, to my organization, for all I can tell to the Reel itself, though I generally keep "patriotism" like that to myself, if I bother to consult it at all. At any rate, once I find my troublemaker, the rest of what I've got to do is comparatively simple; most of the girls, after all, know reasonably well what it is they're getting into, and they seem quite willing to go along with me and to collect what are, in fact, pretty substantial commissions. I believe I'm currently paying higher rates than anyone else on the Reel, and, while there are those who say I do it only because I have to, I prefer to think that at least a few of my reasons are different. Softer, it might be, or more feminine. I am, as you know, a woman—though there are certainly those who doubt it.

People will tell you (if you speak to the right people—that is, of course, from my point of view, the wrong ones) that Marge Sunday isn't a woman at all—and a few of them might even go far enough to tell you that she isn't a human being. As I understand the gossip, I'm supposed to be some sort of robot (you understand I'm giving you the worst of the stories) with a taste for what people call perversions, and an ineradicable hatred for all members of the true human race itself.

But you must remember that you'll hear such things about any person who commands a certain amount of power. And power, in a way, is my business—though it may be simpler if I call it sex.

I run twenty houses of various kinds, a good many of them nothing more than the "straight" or "normal" variety, or whatever, in fact, your word might be for the simple physical pairing of men and women. I hire the girls for some houses, the men for a few others, and I keep them all in line, keep my twenty houses running smoothly, take care of beefs from the tourists, and watch, always, for the troublemaker I mentioned. There really does seem to be one in every new batch, just as if it were a law.

It isn't, of course. Not on the Reel.

There's nothing here that anyone could even call a law. Which helps to make my job, as you might guess, a little simpler. Back in the Comity I might have been forced to spend time and money and energy squaring a beef for some tourist up on his points, but out here I have only to ask him one question. Who is he going to beef to? (Naturally, I don't put it all that baldly to him, but the meaning is clear enough, and I find it sinks in after a very short while. It's Marge Sunday and people like Marge Sunday who run the Reel, and tourists, as a rule, get used to that fact easily enough.)

Beefs don't come up so very often, either; my girls and my men are well trained; I see to that, you may be sure. This current batch was female, ten girls from eighteen to twenty-eight, two of them born right here on the Reel. (Our birth rate, when I come to think of it, must be very nearly the lowest in the occupied universe.) The others, beyond our personal two, had been brought in by traders, or had drifted into my line of work after a start as tourists: it's really surprising how much money you can lose on the Reel if you work at it for a week or two, and how much you can spend, what with one thing and another, even if you don't head for the gaming tables. And then of course there's Willard and his entertainments: a fair number of our lower-class employees start out as tourists hooked by Willard, and end up with me. Though not even Willard has suggested that I pay him a per-head commission.

They were waiting in my office, all ten of them, when I got there; my staff had seen to that, the same staff that had provided me with background scatter on the girls. I ask for efficiency, I train for it, I pay for it and I very generally get it; of course there are penalties if I don't, and the thought of those penalties helps some, too. The office is a neat gray place, big enough to hold twenty people or more, but not gaudy: why waste flash on the employees? And of course the girls were all standing; there is one chair in that office, and the chair belongs to me. I worked hard enough for it.

I opened the door and shut it, and by that time ten girls were watching me nervously, and the smell of perfume, cheap and expensive, clouded the room like a visible haze. I said, "I'm Marge Sunday," and went over to my chair, behind the big polished desk I keep for show, and sat down. You might have heard a pin drop; I've often thought of dropping one, at that moment in the interview, and finding out for certain. But the effect would probably be disappointing; everything else is.

A few seconds passed while nobody said anything, so I went on: "I'll want to know your names."

A girl in her early twenties—brownette hair cut short and curly, tight trim figure in shorts and a skintight blouse, and an expression that tried to be hard and only seemed anxious—said, almost at once, "My name's Marta Dorsay." A thin, hopeful voice, not much class.

I ignored her, flicked my eyes over the group and said, "Your true names. They won't pass this room unless they have to. But they're necessary to me." It was a true statement: any girl who would hold out on a name would go on holding out. This was my first and simplest method of identifying a troublemaker.

The brownette's voice was even thinner and not so hopeful; she shifted inside her clothing. "Shirley Deaks," she said.

"That's better," I told her, and gave her a smile. It seemed just as well to add to her confidence a little, now that she had begun to open herself. "Where are you from, Shirley?" I asked, just as if I had no idea.

"Roentgen," she said, and stopped. It didn't explain anything: most worlds have enough variety among their people to provide the timid and the brave, the ones with resources and the ones without, the tourists and those smart and useless ones who stay at home. But her single word gave me an opening.

"My name is Miss Sunday."

She swallowed, hard, once, and shifted a little more. "Yes, Miss Sunday," she said. "I'm sorry."

I smiled at her again. "I'm not going to have you killed, Shirley. Not unless you deserve it." My eyes went over the group again. "Now, who's next?"

"Christie Chesson."

A good voice, that one, open and warm—a trifle high, but that might have been mere nervousness. I looked for her and found her, gazing at me: a blonde, hair cut like a cap, old-fashioned girlie clothing, skirt and all, over a slim figure with a good straight stance. Intelligent and perhaps even educated. "My name's Miss Sunday," I said again.

"And mine is Miss Chesson. My real name." She didn't look as if she frightened easily, and she didn't look as if she would break with the first touch. I nodded to show that I'd heard her.

"All right, Christie," I said. "Where are you from?"

"Earth."

I didn't remind her again. I'd scored once, and she'd scored once, but there is never any sense in an argument that might be lost: I pick my fights with care. "What brought you here?"

She shrugged. There was nothing obviously enticing about her, but the materials were there; good expensive materials, too. Earth with its very special pride, the old original center, the home of everything, though it was the first Triumvirate that started even the Comity, and the Triumvirate met on Venus E; and Earth never had anything much like the Reel, I can tell you. A few halfhearted first tries, maybe.

This was old Earth, breeding and stance and power, and this girl was going to be very good, very very good. After she'd been broken, of course; and I could manage that.

Meanwhile, she was using that fine voice. "I wanted to see the Reel," she told me. "I'd heard a lot about it."

"You've seen it."

Her tone made the place sound unimportant, even now. "It's an expensive place."

"People like me make it expensive," I said. "And people like you."

"Like me?" That surprised her, if nothing else did: I could see as much in her eyes. But her voice was perfectly flat and calm, entirely controlled. I think I knew then how frightened she truly was; if she hadn't been, after all, she would hardly have needed that much control.

I explained it to her. "Once you've been trained, of course."

"Oh," she said. "Of course." This time it was the girl who gave the smile to me, a small and meaningless motion of the mouth, an acknowledgment I didn't have to care for. I returned it, and we both became, once more, normal.

"What sort of work do you think you ought to be doing?" The others were waiting, but I decided to let them fidget. This Christie needed solving, and there is never any time like the present; I wait when I have to, and only then.

But she gave me little enough help. "I didn't really think you'd ask me." There was no smile now; she held herself steady, waiting, though I wasn't sure either that I knew what she waited for, or that she did.

"I'm asking you," I said, pleasantly enough. "We run our businesses as well as we can for everyone concerned." A lie, of course, and nothing more: troublemakers aren't exactly given their choice of assignment. Neither is anyone else, by the way, not in Marge Sunday's group. It's Marge makes the rules, and it's Marge makes all the rules. No exceptions, and no excuses; everything is run one way, and run right.

She shrugged again, not a bad motion. In its way an appealing motion. It stuck in my mind, not arrogance, not even pride, but assurance, simply that. "I don't really want to do this, you know."

"All right," I said, "what would you like to be doing?" Of course she gave me the expected answer, with a grin that flashed on and off like a blinker come-on, perhaps the first honest expression I'd seen from her. "Flying back to Earth."

"I'm afraid we don't have subsidies, either," I said, and left it there. The grin turned into a grimace and she bounced the ball back in a hurry:

"Of course not; that's how you get your employees, isn't it? Or is 'employee' the proper word?"

The others were definitely nervous now, and I pushed a little propaganda across the desk, into the empty air. "Our employees are happy with us. In every field—"

She cut me off in a voice like withering stone. "Gambling," she said. "Drinking. Drugs. Sex—"

It was my turn to shrug, to act unconcerned. Her pain didn't bother me and her scorn was something I knew all about: tourists usually felt that way about the Reel, even while they used her. There isn't any accounting for tourist feelings, and they never become important enough to matter; only the facts are important, only the truth of the Reel. Which is what I told her: "They're important to people."

"Are they?"

The answer was obvious enough. "If they weren't, the Reel wouldn't exist, not as it is." But there has never been a way to explain the facts of life to a tourist; you might as well try tensor calculus in a kindergarten.

"Or are they just substitutes for something else?" she asked me. I was tired of the argument, tired of talking to this Christie; I'd found my troublemaker, and that part of the job was over. I heard myself going on, but I determined to cut matters short:

"Like what, Christie?"

"Like love—Marge," she told me. "Like love."

The insult was calculated, and I ignored it, which was the only right and proper thing to do. As for the rest of it—well, I'd heard Earthers go sentimental before, and I suppose they do it because they have time to spare, all the time they need to indulge that sort of luxury. We didn't, not on the Reel; we had to face facts, and get to know them, and learn to live through their effects. The words she'd used were no more than words, and all of her talk was no more than a pattern in the air; she didn't know the things themselves, only the words for them. Love was a word to her, too, of course—but there she was like every other person in the universe: love is no more than a word to anybody. There is no thing called love, there is only the sound of the word and the sentiment and the hope—for which a working place like the Reel has neither the time nor the attention; we leave that sort of nonsense to the tourists. It comes in handy as a sales pitch, but it doesn't exist anywhere, in any way. Ask me—or ask my girls, for that matter; we're in the business.

Give her a few months, in fact, and ask this Christie, this Chesson girl. Just provide her with a chance to find out what different kinds of love there are, if that's the word she wants to go on using for a simple fact. And what different sorts of people there are to engage in that simple fact. There are more than you think, I guarantee you that—more, and worse.

And Christie, I told myself finally, was going to one of the worst. I had it all picked out for her. A place where she'd meet the ones she might think of as the lowest of the low, with her old Earth pride, until she got used to some facts. Until she started to become a fact herself, like the rest of us.

That was what I told myself, and that was what I planned. It very nearly worked—and what went wrong was beyond my control.

It had to be, of course. I'm Marge Sunday. And Marge Sunday helps to run the Reel, and she doesn't make mistakes.

Got that?

THIRD CALL

CHAPTER 5

Illusions commend themselves to us because they save us pain and allow us to enjoy pleasure instead. We must therefore accept it without complaint when they sometimes collide with a bit of reality against which they are dashed to pieces.

—from "Reflections on War and Death,"
by Sigmund Freud

ALEX YONGE

CHAPTER 6

That night, my father sent for me. I thought it just as well to obey his order, though there was no necessity compelling me to do so; there isn't, in fact, any such idea as necessity on Three, except, naturally enough, for true physical law. But my father owned the casinos, and the laws of inheritance that do exist on some of the other worlds mean nothing at all to us, though we know of them; we get enough travelers, enough tourists, after all, from every other planet, since there's something for everyone on Three. (That might almost be a slogan, you see: something for everyone. Though it does leave out such types as moralists: the only commodity we don't either provide or peddle is a system of morals, since we haven't so much as got one for our own—which, of course, makes us unique. Every few spins, some traveler comes through to try here one system or another, and he's the only sort of tourist we'd like to boot off. Naturally, we do no such thing—having no facilities for making such an action legal—but the population here, in general, seems just too busy or too smart to pay much attention to a system that does anything but increase the nightly take. The unfortunate traveler usually ends by complaining that the rest of us are too busy; the rest of us prefer to say we're too smart, and, I suppose, you can make your own choice of excuse.)

Father held a suite over the main gaming room, and I went up the private staircase with a bodyguard to show me the path—which is not, by the way, what I've heard tourists call conspicuous consumption. We keep a staff on retainer, of course, and we've got to—if there's nothing else for them to do they take over servant's duties for a few of us—but anything truly conspicuous is for the tourists, not for us. We're practical men here on Three, practical and serious.

Does it surprise you, by the way (does, in fact, such a realization surprise the Undersecretary?) that I know as much as I do seem to know about the way other worlds operate, and about the theories they discuss, the structures in which they believe? The explanation, simply enough, is just this: that I do a lot of listening. And it has always seemed to us a valuable thing to be able to answer a tourist, when necessary, or to reassure him as indicated, in his own language—language being, of course, a great deal more than a mere matter of words.

(We haven't got a language of our own here; of course, there's no need for it. We use Standard, and it serves our purposes neatly enough.)

I pushed the door open. Father was sitting behind his telltale-desk, which was dark, since there was no action of especial interest taking place downstairs; he looked square at me and asked, "What was the fight about?" The door snapped shut behind me, leaving, naturally enough, the bodyguard outside.

I felt a little worried and a little defiant, like a man with five chips left to lose and no bankroll stacked home. I said, "It wasn't really a fight," and heard my voice echo there with perhaps even a quaver. After all, he was older than I was, more powerful and more influential; he was my father, too. It all meant something to me.

"Don't bother with that," he told me in a flat tone, shifting in his chair but still staring directly at me. "I caught most of it right here on the screen; one of the stickmen flashed red before you hit Frain." He nodded at the tall sidewall of the desk as if he were acknowledging his reflection in that shining blackness; then his eyes came back to me, waiting.

"I didn't realize—"

But the excuse I'd begun for him simply was given no chance to work. "Naturally," he said, "or you wouldn't have tried covering it up with words. Now: what was it all about?" He leaned forward, elbows on the shining top of the desk, and blanked his face to listening.

"He said—" I tried to remember, but it seemed to me then that the fight had happened a long time before, and that, in any case, it hadn't truly been a fight about Frain's insult. But there was nothing else for me to offer. "He said the gaffs were squat. Everybody could see through them, old-fashioned—they couldn't fool even the tourists."

"Do you think he was right?" My father had put on the very tone of his lectures to me, and I told myself I was in for an hour or more of talk. In fact, I couldn't stop myself from feeling more and more guilty, more and more nervous; well, of course, he had the power. He was a big white-haired man with a square and heavy face, and he didn't look old at all, but only resigned, and knowing, and strong. All of that had an effect on me, there's no denying it; I only tried to act, within my nervousness, as well as I might.

"Of course not!" I answered him, trying to sound at the same time honest and surprised.

"Then why bother to fight about it?"

"But he said—"

"Words will never hurt you, Alex." Eyes closed and opened again; he took a breath and I found myself interrupting him.

"He said we had a surprise waiting for us—that, too."

"A surprise?" My father looked expectant, perhaps a little tense, as he waited for me, though in that time he could have known nothing of what was to come to us all.

"He wouldn't say more."

He shook his head. "Did you question him?" he asked me, disapproving. The tone, as well as the words, rattled me a little, adding to nervousness.

"There wasn't—" I began, and then added: "It wasn't any time to—"

The lecturing-tone was now back in his voice. "Another reason, Alex, for restraint in the use of your fists. That's the sort of thing we want to get rid of on the Reel." He used, of course, in conversation, the slang term for our world; but I do try, in such a report as this, to use the proper words for things whenever I can. It seems to me only equally important that I also record speech with accuracy.

"Why?"

"Bad for business, Alex."

But this, of course, was no more than the argument I had examined for myself, and here, I thought, I had at last complete answers. "Is it?" I began. "The customers like local color—"

"They do until it hits them," he said flatly.

"I was hitting Frain," I answered. "Nobody else."

He nodded once. "And Frain staggered off. He might just as well have bounced into some tourist—from Prossy, or Earth, or any place at all. And when the local color begins to involve the tourists, that's when the tourists stop liking it. They want to be excited, but they want to be safe, too."

Such an attitude seemed to me nonsense, and I said so; it was like wanting to be with a girl and never touch her. Of course there are some tourists that odd, but it was hard for me to believe they represented any large number.

"I didn't say it wasn't silly," my father went on. "But tourists—all of them, very nearly—are like that. Believe a man who's had experience, Alex—and I've had a fairly wide range of that."

"I suppose you're right." I didn't argue, or become excited; we pride ourselves on our calm, here on Three, and we remain calm whenever in honor we can. Tourists maintain enough excitement for all of us.

"Now," he said, as if he wanted simply to return to a subject of true importance, "what did this surprise sound like? Goon squad?"

I tried to remember, and realized that Frain clearly could not have been thinking of anything so simple, so usual as that. "Something else," I said at last. "Something new."

"Any ideas, then?"

I shook my head. "He sounded awfully sure of himself, Father."

He heard, undoubtedly, the fright and the uncertainty in my voice, and spoke firmly: "I don't doubt he was—but that doesn't mean he was justified."

"Of course not." But, as I reminded myself even then, it didn't mean he wasn't, either.

I'm simply not certain why Frain had made me so nervous; at the time, after all, I knew nothing about his plans, or about those who were his assistants and his masters. But there was a man named Diamond, who spoke with Frain that night; I was not present at that talk, and I have never heard the words they used, though I set down here what the conversation must have been like; let it, then, aid you in understanding what was then our present and our future, and is now our present and our past.

Diamond asked, simply, "Is everything ready?"

"We'll be set in forty-eight hours."

"That's a long time for me to wait," Diamond said. They spoke, somewhere, alone and hidden, in quiet tones and rapidly; I know no more than that.

"You want to be sure, don't you?"

"Of course I do," Diamond said. "But—two days—"

"It's a big grab. There's no sense missing it, just to hurry it along."

"You're right; but if it can be hastened—"

"We'll do what we can," Frain said. "No promises. I'm as anxious as you are, remember."

"I suppose you are," Diamond said. "I heard about that."

"About what?"

"The fight."

Frain shook his head. "The fight's nothing. But I'd like . . ." He stopped, as if to think or to imagine.

"Of course you would," Diamond said impatiently. "And I'll give you the chance. Don't worry about that."

"I'm not worried," Frain said.

"We depend on each other," Diamond told him, very slowly and very surely. "For everything. And everything will be repaid: don't doubt it."

"Afterward," Frain said.

"Afterward."

But of course we knew nothing of Diamond, nothing at all. Time was passing while we remained in this ignorance, and very little time was left to run out into our world before Diamond and his plan were upon us.

And—this, too—I was jangled still, nervous from the talk I had suffered, and I took some time away from the tables (as, clearly, I was entitled to do), and went off to try my joy at one of Marge Sunday's establishments, meaning no harm and intending, only, to restore myself with an hour or so of interest and of involvement; nothing more important, nothing, in fact, more meaningful than that.

Yet my attempt at restoration, no less, was the second step. No one could have known, no one could have imagined; but it was so.

FOURTH CALL

CHAPTER 7

"The principal difficulty is that he doesn't know what he wants. The next is that I don't either—or what I want myself. I only know what I don't want," said Miriam brightly, as if she were uttering some happy, beneficent truth. "I don't want a person who takes things even less simply than I do myself."

—from *The Tragic Muse,* by Henry James

DANIEL COLES

CHAPTER 8

"How much?"

I asked him that and he looked at me. A little surprised. "I'll take care of you," he said. He was a middling height, and he looked as if he'd started out to be a thin stick, but he'd rounded out some. Going bald in front, but it gave him a distinguished look. A little mouth, set in one straight line, and eyes that were always looking at something else, not at you. Nothing else special about him.

"I'd like to know," I said.

"Two hundred."

I thought that over. Guild wages for a straight job were seventy-five, but I hadn't taken standard wages for a long time. My own rates ran to a hundred thirty-five, and sixty-five extra wasn't much of a boost. "Five hundred."

"Ridiculous." He used words like that; they didn't mean anything. I looked back at him, but he was a tough one to break.

"You want a good man or you wouldn't have come to me," I said. "Good men get high rates."

"Two fifty."

We settled at three twenty-five, which was all right with me. Three twenty-five was going to feel just fine in the bank account. I told him my name, and he told me that his was Diamond. It didn't make any difference to me what his name was.

"Where do you want me?" I asked him.

"Follow along," he said. "We'll start here and now."

That was all right, too. I don't like a man who wastes time. There's too much waiting to go wrong in any few ticks. A bodyguard is always looking for something to go wrong: it's part of the job. Even a job like this Diamond's offer.

I didn't think we were in any trouble, though. We went down the hall to the building entrance and on out, under the arch with its motto and the colored permanent chemostat pics. When we were out on the street he turned right and I followed a pace or so behind, trying to outguess him.

Most of the girlie houses were to the left, and a fair percentage of the gambling palaces. Out to the right were money changers and salesmen and a string of needle joints, and at the end of the track a scatter of hotels. I couldn't make up my mind, so I went along watching the crowds. We passed some people I knew, but nobody to say hello to. It wasn't a long walk, not what I'd call long.

We stopped in front of a jewelry sales shop, and he looked back at me. "You'd better come along."

I'd have done that without words. I didn't waste any on him. We went in and the little man behind the counter looked up. I'd seen him around.

"What is it?" he said. He looked at Diamond and paid me no attention at all.

"I'm here to buy," Diamond said.

The man behind the counter shook his head. He was small and old, white-haired and a little tense. His eyes kept moving, flicking back and forth as if he didn't know what might come out of the walls. The walls weren't his worry. "The place isn't for sale," he said.

"I'll pay you a fair price."

"It isn't enough," the old man said. "I want to keep the place running."

"I won't shut it down," Diamond said.

"I'll have nothing to do. I need to keep active."

"Relax. Retire. Go somewhere else."

"After the Reel? There isn't anywhere else. I've been here seventy years."

It didn't sound like a long time, the way he said it. Diamond said, "I'll be taking over. Your place, every place."

"I've been independent all my life," the old man said.

"Things change."

"I don't change. I'm running my own place, and I'll go on."

"You're sure?" Diamond said.

"I'm sure."

Diamond took his eyes off the old man and looked at me instead. "Go ahead," he told me.

I don't like beam work. It cuts through and hurts too many bystanders. Here, it could have messed up the shop. I showed the old man my slug gun.

He said, "And—don't—"

Diamond said, "Go ahead."

The old man said, "I'll pay you more—whatever he pays—" but I wasn't truly listening. I squeezed the trigger and he fell over behind the counter. After the echoes had died away we moved the body out back.

Diamond said, "I'll stay here until my man arrives."

"All right."

"I've got somebody to run the place. I've got enough people to run every place on the Reel."

"All right," I said. It didn't matter to me.

He paid me in cash and I put the revolver away and went out. After I'd stacked the cash into my bank I told myself I had a vacation coming and I headed over to Marge Sunday's party. I knew where it was running; it's one of the things I'm interested in.

The thought of that three twenty-five was a good one. When I've got enough money I'll move off the Reel and head in for a nice peaceful place. Maybe I'll have a girl of my own by that time.

I didn't wonder about what Diamond had told me. He hadn't paid me for that.

FIFTH CALL

CHAPTER 9

"Is that not the secret aim of every man and woman," he thought, "to find in his friend the abiding countenance of calm, the continual, even flow of feeling? This is the norm of love, and no sooner do we deviate from it, change or grow cold, than we suffer; therefore, my ideal is everyone's ideal. Is that not the crowning achievement, the solution of the relations between the sexes? To give passion a lawful outlet, to direct its course, like a river, for the benefit of the whole community—that is the common problem of mankind; it is the very pinnacle of progress, toward which all of the George Sands strive, invariably losing their way. Once it is solved, there will be no heart, and, consequently, a perpetually rich, full life and perpetual moral health."

—from *Oblomov,* by Ivan Goncharov,
translated by Ann Dunnigan

ALEX YONGE

CHAPTER 10

She came over toward me, a stranger, a new girl, and I heard her voice before I saw her there; I was, I imagine, staring somewhere else, thinking about something or other, not yet, so early in the evening, totally relaxed. But when she spoke I did hear her, and turned to see her. "Want to talk a while? You look like an interesting person."

It was then I turned and got a snap of her, a tall, heavyset girl with long blonde hair and a face that looked, somehow, sadder than the smile she wore on it, the smile she was wearing, quite deliberately of course, for me and for that moment; in its way, in fact, an interesting face, but not quite my type. Not just then. "Sorry," I said, as nicely as I might.

"It's okay." Her voice was deep and a little hoarse, part of the character she used, and for a second her face smiled more widely at me, before she turned away to look for someone else, someone more complaisant; of course, all that about my being an interesting person was come-on and no more than come-on, but I appreciated it even while I knew the limits of its reality; Marge's parties were always good ones.

I had a drink in my hand, because someone had, at some time, simply put it there; but I wasn't using it for anything, merely holding it and not quite realizing the fact. Somehow, in spite of the place and the company,

I was still worried, still keyed up. I kept thinking of Frain and of his threat, and the very vagueness of it was beginning to bother me. I made, even, the foolish mistake of a tourist, and tried to relax, but, as anyone knows, trying never works: I remained tense, as strung as a tourist and very nearly as stupid. I kept looking round the room as if, somewhere, the key that would unlock me sat waiting for me to notice it.

There was a man in a far corner whom I knew slightly, a big man with the shaven head of a bodyguard; his name was Coles and we'd hired him for a temporary hook several years before. A good man, and a solid professional, as far as I remembered him, but he looked something other than professional at Marge Sunday's; everyone was different in that atmosphere. There was the hell of a lot of noise.

Her parties had always been available and inviting for me to relax in, providing always an air in which I could forget for the moment anything that was going wrong outside the rooms, forget, in fact, that I maintained anything resembling a position to uphold or a plan to carry out, and simply, within the walls of the party, become myself, whatever that happened to be (and I had been frankly surprised now and again). There were stimulants distributed for anyone who wanted them, anything in existence from light alcohols to heavy needlework, but (in spite of the drink in my hand) I had seldom enough indulged in anything of that sort; I was, when I thought about it, a lucky sort of person, able simply to relax when I had to, in circumstances that permitted it, without being forced into drugging or dosing. I have heard various people tell me they like the taste of liquor, but that seems to me a fairly obvious excuse for a necessity—one which, thanks to heredity-plus, has never been a necessity for me.

And here was the atmosphere I had wished for: lights and noise, shadows and the general sense of carefree freedom; a mixture I can't truly describe to you except in such vague terms, an excitement taken raw and at the same time a calm that overlay everything else the way the smoke of the place overlay the clarity of air, the brittle sound of glass and the deeper, freer noise of laughter there, all in motion without hurry or tension, some of us bunched into crowds that heaved and shifted, some alone, in pairs, groups, drifting variously, talking, touching, accepting, making, of all the materials of such a place and time, use and comfort, freedom and ease—all of it sprung free and loud. There were no tourists, not there: off the beaten track, in rooms maintained and quieted, we were ourselves, and we wanted no real strangers around, no explanations, no demands. Except for Marge's people, of course, the boys and girls who were, after all, the main entertainment; if entertainment is the word.

Coles was talking to a small girl who wore a bright orange magnetic shift and an eager expression; his hands went up and down in the smoky air as he described something to her, and her head nodded vigorously, as if whatever he described were the most fascinating thing in the world; the smoke did nothing, suddenly, to hide the trained and necessary quality of her response, and the room seemed to me gradually more and more false, empty and hollow; so I knew, and told myself, that I was in bad shape.

Of course the party was a fake; but what difference did that of necessity make to me? Everything, if you see it the right way, is a falsity: we none of us do what we mean (since, in obedience to profit and privilege, we can't) or say what we mean (since, in threat and obedience, we don't dare) or in truth act at all except under the impress of one form or another of profit; and, as clearly as I've ever been able to see, that goes as well for your religious-addiction types and your reformers as well, though you have first to define a word like "profit" a little differently. The rule is, then, to forget the fake when it doesn't involve you directly, and jerk out of the world as much profit, as much good-time, as you can; it's a good rule, in fact, and a good way to live, a satisfying, free and even way of walking through your time. But when you lose your grip on it, as I'd lost, momentarily, mine, there's nothing left. Nothing at all, to hold me up.

Frain had disturbed me more than I'd thought, possibly because he'd disturbed, as much, my father; I could understand that much of my own trouble, and I didn't like it. I kept thinking that my father was hardly the man to accept disturbance over any matter which was truly small.

I kept thinking . . . and the girl with Dan Coles laughed, a high, delighted sound I could hear even over the rest of the party's noise. The lights, then, dimmed and brightened, and on that signal most of us became quiet, and Marge Sunday climbed up on a table, holding loose-fisted a dark bottle (she never drank, she was a quiet woman of business and arrangement, but the bottle she held, her open stance on the table, all of it added to the loose, the free feeling of the place and time; it was all false, my mind kept saying, all false, and nothing made any difference), and she looked round at us as we waited, sitting, leaning, standing and sprawled.

"Everybody's having a good time," she said at last in that loud, flat, no-nonsense voice we all knew well. "And that's fine. Because that's what these parties are for, and you all know that. I've just got a couple of announcements to make."

She stopped and in the silence somebody laughed, a high, uncontrolled sound that might have been male or female and had, in any case, nothing to do with her words. She waited for the sound to die away and then shrugged at us, which drew from the crowd a new, but a small, laugh; and then she went on.

"There's a Null Lounge set up in the back today. I don't have to tell you any more than that; null work is expensive, but it's a pleasure to pay for, it's worth it. Whoever you're with will take care of that."

She got a little spatter of cheers, and again she waited, and again, after a second or two of silence, went on. She was good at her job; it was only Alex Yonge who kept seeing it as a job, as a fake; except for me, the place was happy, the place was free.

"And there's a workout set, too, downstairs and entirely soundproofed. I don't think we need anything truly special here, so outside of the workout crew, which is down there right now waiting for customers, these are just my regular people. No costuming, no flag, no age specialties; you're not tourists with a life's worth of hates to work off. We're all together here and we're all part of the Reel: just relax and have yourselves a space in time."

She waved the bottle and laughed and got off the table, disappearing into the clots and clusters of the crowd, and the place began to buzz again with talk and motion, the lights flicked all the way down to dim and stayed there, and I was seated, quiet, afraid and alone.

There seemed nothing for me; the Null Lounge needed a partner and I had no desire to hunt a partner for a free-fall foolery of whatever sort. And the workout group would have done nothing for me; unless you can pose a situation for them, cast them in it and have the situation played the way you wanted it instead of the way it happened, what's the point?

And I'd won the fight, of course. How could I, even with a workout group, in privacy and imagination, revise that and relax?

It simply wasn't, as I was beginning to realize, a slice of time with my name on it. Everyone gets the deeps now and again, and I had them, down as far as the core and colored blue-black as the stratosphere; but nothing more serious than the deeps had happened, I kept telling myself; there isn't any cure for such feelings, but they pass, they take their place in the past parade before too many ticks have gone by.

Thoughts like that, naturally enough, were very little comfort to me; I was stuck in the groove of mood, and I knew it: no party, no filled space or whirling time, was going any way at all to lift me up.

Then, of course, I saw her.

Let me stop time for a second and show you the picture I had of her in that first second: here. She was no peanut, no tiny-girl, but she was no giant, either, nothing like the tall one who'd cut into me before. This girl was a blonde, too, and had that much in common with the other; her hair, though, was straight, capcut, and her eyes were a very direct and visible blue. She had a skin that didn't stretch, spot or sag, and a figure as straight as a stalk. Just the middle height, she was, turned away from me a little, and I swear I knew what her voice was like before she spoke, before, in fact, even, she saw me.

She caught me looking, then, and came over through a crowd that made casual way for her, as if she weren't special at all. She'd been doing nothing but letting her eyes flick from one to one: a new girl, I saw, one who hadn't been at a party for us before; but I couldn't imagine Marge wasting her on the tourists. I sat where I was, and forgot all that other, and I waited for her to arrive.

But even that didn't seem right of me, suddenly; as if, in fact, she weren't a girl at all but a person.

Silly. She said softly, "Looking for me?"

"I'd like to talk for a while." I hadn't known I was prepared to use those words, or any words. Relax and flow free, was what the party said to me, and for a second, there and then, I'd had hold of the idea. But nervousness came back quickly enough, and something else and something new came with it.

"My name's Christie Chesson," she said, in the voice I already knew; it was neither a good voice nor a bad one, but familiar, and for that reason easing, and frightening as well.

"Alex Yonge." My own voice sounded a little strange, as if, somehow, she were the known person and I the other.

"I'm new here." And that was no excuse, possibly not even an explanation, but a fact, a sentence tossed like a tie line, no more.

"I know that."

"Oh," she said, and then: "You come here often?" It seemed to me that I needed to explain myself to her, needed, in fact, to justify what of course required no justification, but her eyes were very strange.

"I try to relax," I said. "Some days it isn't any good."

There was a short silence after that had been spoken out, and I believe that neither of us moved. She said suddenly, "I don't know how I'm supposed to act now."

"It doesn't matter," I told her, surprised, perhaps, to notice that what I had said seemed to me true: I had, it appeared, neither demands nor needs at that moment; I find that I can't describe what it was I did feel.

"You shouldn't be tense," she said.

"I'm not tense." And that, too, might have been true: I was frightened, but at ease; I understood neither myself nor anyone or anything else.

She asked me, then, quietly and calmly, as if she were as familiar to me as her voice, "Is this the way it usually is?"

I had a reply for her, a reply which cut away instantly the last of the wall between us, the wall of her profession and my standing, and which recognized that wall at the same time, recognized its strength and, in spite of invisibility, its permanence: "This isn't a way it can be."

"I know," she said.

"I suppose you do."

"We both do."

"Christie—" I began, but she stopped me.

"No. Not yet."

I was willing that she be right; I said, after a second, "Let's talk, then."

She remained standing over me; I remained seated, the glass in my hand; but the room seemed very silent. "I ran out of money," she told me steadily. "I was silly and stupid. I've got to pay for it this way."

"I can take you out of—"

"Not yet," she said, and I stopped. But after a silence began again. "Say my name."

"Not that, either," she told me, with perfect certainty. "This is where we are." The picture remained in my mind, the idea that I was the stranger, she the familiar one, she the known and I the new.

"Christie—"

"I don't know you yet," she told me. "I can't be sure."

I needed, then, her knowledge; it was the first of my needs. "I've been stupid," I said. "My father—he's got power. I will have." There was no way to explain to her what I had to explain; but she may, even then, have understood. "I don't know how to handle it. I've got to be taught. I've got to be helped."

"I have nothing anymore," she said. "You know that."

"It doesn't matter."

"It has to matter." She sounded more sure of herself than I could sound; it was as if she knew the world we were in, and I knew, only, the world in which I lived and to which, so very accidentally, she had come.

"I'll see you again," I offered.

"Whenever you like." And she emphasized in those words, once more, her position, and mine, so that the wall rose between us again, visible and tangible, and created its silence.

After which I asked, "There isn't anything to talk about, is there?"

"We've talked already."

"We've said nothing."

"It's too soon," she told me. "I don't know—" But it was my turn to explain, my turn, even, to sound assured, and to become certain.

"You know."

"I can't—"

"We'll begin, then," I said. "Just begin." And in the silence of that noisy room, in the light of that dimness, I stirred, and stood, and spoke one word, and she replied; we had, by that, begun.

"Christie."

"Alex."

SIXTH CALL

CHAPTER 11

"His upbringing?" Bazarov exclaimed. "Every man should educate himself—well, just as I did, for example . . . As to the time, why should I depend on them? Much better they should depend on me. No, brother, all that is just loose thinking, there's nothing solid behind it! And what are these mysterious relations between men and women? We physiologists, we know what sort of relations those are. Just study the anatomy of the eye: how is one to explain that mysterious glance, as you term it? It's all sheer romanticism, stuff and nonsense, putrefaction, artiness. Let us rather go and examine our beetle."

—from *Fathers and Sons,* by Ivan Turgenev,
translated by George Reavy

MARGARET SUNDAY

CHAPTER 12

She didn't make too much of a fight for me, but of course she didn't like it much, either; even I couldn't have expected that.

Understand me: we run a service business here, or what's called a service business, and if you live somewhere else, on some other world, you may have used the words a good many times and never thought of what a "service business" really might be. Oh, there are firms virtually everywhere with that sort of name plastered over them, organizations that sell you a procedure or an event instead of a product or a package, and if you think at all it's that sort of thing you think about. But here on the Reel we're a little bit special.

Just like anyone else anywhere, we've got to give the customer what he wants in order to make out for ourselves: no matter how you slice it, if you want to cop the cap you've got to check the choice. But there's an old saying that's come true for us, and it's this: the customer doesn't know what he wants. We've got to tell him—and then give it to him.

In the early days, oh, before I was around to peer and profit, there were tests and surveys, personality-pattern-profiles and project-projectives, you name it and we had some of it, a veritable pile of paper poking the sky out. And, all of it said and done and over with, what good did we get from our garbage? None whatever, naturally enough; questions give you no more than the answers people are somehow, someway, willing to hand out, and depth surveys give you results so very general that you're still stuck with no reply when you come down to this person, this time, this place. Oh, we had statistics to the ceiling, extrapolated curves to the corners of the universe; what we didn't have, we discovered very slowly, was anything we could use, anything we could handle.

Besides, there's this: the Reel changes people. There's a lot they think they want, and when they find out they're free to have it (and on the Reel free is what they are, for anything at all) the freedom is enough; they don't have to have what they wanted anymore, don't have to buy it, don't have to make a capful of profit for us on it; the freedom is enough.

It's fine for them, but not-so-good for us: right?

Now, my business hooks itself up with a fair number of others—the needle trades, for instance, and the drink pressers. And those businesses, and a lot of others, were doing surveys of their own. (All this was in my mother's time, the end of it at any rate; I've heard the stories and seen the materials, but I'm not so old as all that. Not yet I'm not.) After a time we had, all of us, enough paper and enough graphwork to cover the planet and wrap it in ribbons.

So we stopped.

And we started, then and there, providing anything-and-everything. If you want it, if you can dream it up, and if—important—you can pay for it . . . it's yours. The Reel provides, three cheers for the Reel. Right?

That went on for about ten years. And by the end of that ten years we had a fair idea of what most people were going to ask for. (Oh, we still get the occasional oddity, but then we're prepared for oddities now; if you can dream it up, we can mock it up, take your exchange and make it worth your while.) The Null Lounge idea caught on and became a Marge Sunday specialty; the workout crews were a general notion, and everybody's using them now. But of course those two aren't all we have here, not by any manner of means: I run an extensive chain. People want a great many different things.

Mostly, what they want is release. They call it pleasure, but people have a habit of putting the wrong names to things (like "service business," for instance, which is what we have here on the Reel and what other people think they have on other, and dreamier, worlds), and you can take my word for it: the word is "release." After all, why should sex

—just sex itself, without the frills and specialties—be such a big item for us here?

We're built to provide what the customer can't get at home, what with moralities and laws and the various neuroses of various public figures—and he can certainly get sex at home. That's where new customers come from, right?

But the sex he gets at home (and it's a pleasure, naturally; it always is) isn't a release. Everything he does is all tied up with rules and regulations, the do's and the don'ts of fifty thousand planets. Morality. Structure. Law. Habit. All the same, and all a trap.

So he wants to feel free. He wants to feel release. And he comes to the Reel. Simplicity itself.

Once he's released, though—once he gets that first taste of air on the Reel, and makes up his mind for true that nobody is watching him, not even himself—then he's likely to start experimenting. Things he didn't think of, back home. Or things he did think of, and never dared to try.

That's a new kind of release for him. At home, they wouldn't stand for it. But on the Reel, all it takes is a little exchange.

Now, I don't mean the luxury trade—not the Null Lounge sort of affair. That's games-playing, and frills, and excitement, but it's a luxury.

Most of my special trade is made up of necessities. Give a man a new oddity in the way of sex (or a woman, for that matter; there's less difference than you might think, if you come from a place like Earth) and you've given him an addiction. He doesn't exactly want it anymore: now, he needs it.

Facts like that are handy for the Reel. The necessity trade makes up a fair percentage of our business.

And when I put the proposition to Christie, naturally enough, she didn't take to it. Very few do, and the ones who take to it fastest are usually the worst for the job: enthusiasm takes the place of judgment, and the customer doesn't get what he wants.

I'm in the business, remember. People tend to kid themselves along through life, people who (like the old remaining Earth originals) don't have to hardscrabble for a decent living, people who are too soft to take the sort of proposition the Reel turns out to be. People tend to believe in sentiment, for instance, and all sorts of "human values" and "depth relationships."

None of this cackle actually exists; I've told you that and shown you why, right?

But people do believe it. Especially Earth types, like Christie. It takes a while for the idea of a specialty job to sink in.

"I went to the party—" she said, very defensively. Telling me she understood her job, and did it. She'd had her clothes yanked, but she was too smart to complain about that. She didn't like being tied up, though, like a side of meat on display; but she'd get used to that, too.

She wasn't a bad-looking type. The Earth genes mark for quality, and she had that. A sort of dignity. Which is only a word and an attitude, anyhow, but it's something the tourists will pay for.

Oh, she was going to be good. "And you sat around and talked," I told her. "I was watching you: believe that."

She tried to heave at the ropes, but those ties weren't made to break for girls like Christie. She relaxed, as much as she could in that position, and tried defending herself again. I imagine she thought I was punishing her. "I was doing my job," she told me flatly. No tears and no whine. What I said: dignity. "Or I think I was, anyhow."

We don't punish people. We train them. "You were supposed to be circulating," I told her.

"If someone just wants to talk—"

Time. I stepped forward and hit her. The flat of my hand, but she bounced back in her ropes and hissed a breath full to the lungs. "I saw you," I said. "You weren't just talking."

She spent a second getting breath to answer with. "We were—"

"Do you think I'm new at this? Do you think I haven't seen everything there is to see?"

She took it, color coming back into her face now. The private clock in my head ticked out another second before she said, quite evenly and with more calm than I might have expected, "What are you going to do with me?"

"I'm going to send you to a special group," I said. "I've told you that. After you're trained . . . There are lots of odd ways people get their kicks."

She looked at me and didn't say anything. Time: I hit her again and this time she made no sound at all. Self-contained. Tough. But she'd break; I was going to see to that.

I had to see to it, after all. It was my job.

And no more than my job, get that straight.

After a time I went on. "I was going to assign you to a special group from the first," I told her. "But I wanted to see you work out, just once, at a normal party. Background, right?"

"I did my best—" But it still wasn't pleading: no more than defense. There was pain, but she didn't let the pain sell her a thing. A hard one, under all that smooth-and-soft: quality. Call it that.

"You'll do better in the next group. Four girls, on assignment. Actually, it's less working time." I always try to give them a motive for the job: a motive helps. I want no runaways, nothing of that sort to take up my time.

"I don't care—"

Time. I was picking my spots and I knew she hurt, so I used the pain; if she wouldn't buy it, it was up to me to sell it to her. "When you're hit that's all you can think about," I told her. I did it again, a little harder, and this time I got a sound out of her, high-pitched and lasting not a fifth of a second. "You'll forget him, believe me; there won't be room in your head for him. He won't be there." And again.

Her eyes were wet; that was all. Control.

But she'd break. "You won't be hurt much," I told her. "No more than this." And again, until her skin was reddening. Until she breathed a little harder and watched my hand for threat. "We've got static fields that take up most of the punishment. You'll feel it—but not seriously. Not really seriously."

Again. And when she could talk she started to lose that mask. "Sta—static fields . . . wh—wh—"

And that was it: she'd forgotten about her pure-boy, of course, just as I'd told her. Training and action leave no room; you can say what you like about love and about all the romantic words some worlds have time and space to dream of. But love has nothing to do with the lives we live.

Love has nothing to do with the job.

I gave her some more talk while she bit back the weep. "There are a lot of men who like to hurt their girls," I told her. "Before, or instead of; either way. You'll be just right for a group like that." No more than the simple, natural truth, and of course she flamed up at it and started jerking at the ropes again.

"You can't—it's slavery—"

"It's a paying job," I said. "And you need a paying job."

"But—"

I let her take some calm. Resignation, she would have called it. I called it growing up.

Look: she was ready enough to do an ordinary job. Only now, she was hurt, and because she was hurt she was scared. Just scared and nothing more; all that about Yonge was sentiment, and sentiment is only an excuse. She was lying to herself, the way most people do—most people and all tourists—and I was hurting her there, too.

"I'll run away—" she started after a tick or two.

I hit her, and this time I hit her hard, and measured, and left her on the edge of her own control. Teetering. "Where?" I asked her. "And how? Think you can get loose? Think you can get away from me—or from this?" My hand again, just a reminder, but she was sore and tender, and a word gasped out of her lungs:

"Someone—"

"Not on the Reel," I told her. "Not even that newfound pure-boy. He's got troubles of his own, Christie; he's got no time for you. Any more than you have time for him, right now. No room, Christie." I hit her again and she bounced out and moaned, and with the next one she screamed. "No room."

"Please—"

"I won't help you, and he can't," I said. Again. And again. "He's got troubles, too, Christie. Not like yours—" Once more. "But he's got too many troubles to think of where you are, or what I'm doing." And again.

Oh, I'd been hearing a little about Yonge. Just a little, but for me a little was enough.

After all, I've been around. Right?

SEVENTH CALL

CHAPTER 13

CYRANO

Struck down
By the sword of a hero, let me fall—
Steel in my heart, and laughter on my lips!
Yes, I said that once. How Fate loves a jest!—
Behold me ambushed—taken in the rear—
My battlefield a gutter—my noble foe
A lackey with a log of wood . . .
It seems
Too logical—I have missed everything,
Even my death!

RAGUENEAU

(Breaks down.)
Ah, monsieur!—

CYRANO

Ragueneau,

Stop blubbering! *(Takes his hand.)*
What are you writing nowadays,
Old poet?

RAGUENEAU

(Through his tears)
I am not a poet now;
I snuff the—light the candles—for Molière!

—from *Cyrano de Bergerac,* Act V,
by Edmond Rostand, translated
by Brian Hooker

ALEX YONGE

CHAPTER 14

It was afternoon, not that the time made any difference to decision, or to action: we're a sun-round, moon-round world, after all. But the shadows seemed to help, the very stilling and the cooling of the air of afternoon, the very vagueness of the streets and ways in those hours when any act appears all possible, and all acts of equal likelihood. Perhaps we should never have gone out, and I can blame myself for the motion though I know the decision was very little of mine; still, I might have stopped it if I'd thought of the way, and thought the way were needed, and I find some easement only in telling myself, very often as the days go on, that what happened would have happened in any case, in one action or in another, in one room or in another; certainly it was bound and determined to happen, and I wish only that I were full-grown in this respect: that my belief in that fact were as decided as the fact itself.

My father, certainly, was determined for it, determined for the knowledge, in simple fact, of what it was Frain had used for his threat; quite regardless of how that careful man had passed Frain off, he was not the sort to accept, easily, as it were lying down, any such form of words without shaping them into a challenge of his own. In his great office on that afternoon his voice was as calm as if what he discussed had somehow already occurred. "We'll talk to him on his own ground, and force him to disclosure."

"Maybe he was only steaming off," I said. "Maybe the words meant nothing at all, not really."

"Then that's what we discover," he said, and stood, ready and armed to go. We carried weapons in readiness, all of us on Three, though they were seldom enough of real use; but the weapons were our statements and enforcements: we had, and we needed, no others.

I was standing as well, and nearer to the door. "But if he's ready for you—" I began, and my father waved a big hand impatiently, cutting me off with the obvious statement, as if I were entirely a child.

"I'm ready for him as well."

"Are we taking a bodyguard?" I asked him. The suggestion was not too novel; we had used guards on similar missions, and not always simply to protect our money and our goods.

But he shook his head, moving toward the door slowly, so that I stepped back and allowed him to open it into the bright noise of the downstairs Palace. "We'll go alone," he said clearly, over that new sound. "A show of force would push him to the wall; there's no need for that as yet."

And still I was hesitant, though my hesitation had no knowledge to give it weight. "Perhaps—"

"Or I'll go alone," he said, turning back to face me. "That choice, at least, is yours."

The words hung spaced in the air, and of course I ignored the chance they offered, and went with him then, down the stairs and through the gaming rooms themselves, since after all he was my father, and he controlled what was one day to be mine. It was, as I knew, suitable for me to copy his actions thus, and so to learn from him. And yet it was not entirely the power resident in him that pushed my motion: oddly, I wished to see him safe. And after all, it might have been possible for me to protect him. All this was a weakness, as I fully know, and as even then I knew quite well, but it was a weakness I found again and again in myself without any concurrent ability to extirpate it; perhaps, in fact, I have never fully grown up. But why should I bother you with my conscience, when it cannot be of interest to you; when, in fact, you can never truly understand it? Let this stand, in any case: what aid of mine could be provided, was for whatever reason his to command.

And so it was we set out together, past the noise of our own Palace and toward the Palace which Frain kept for his own, and where, my father thought truly, he might be found; we traveled through the districts where the tourists walked in the shadows of that afternoon, where the signs blinked and resolved in the last of daylight, where the hawkers and the traders passed and repassed a skirt's width from our moving selves; at first, there was no one we knew to hail, and yet I peered at the faces, peered at the crowds like a man measuring for his first big jerk-and-take. At last I realized that I was searching, in my weakness, for the face of the girl, Christie, whom I had seen the night before, the girl who would certainly not be out, nor even free, so early in her training (she had been quite new, I realized that; and yet I stared now)—and for whom, in the end, I had no business in looking. My guilt lies in that, too; and my inattention received example and correction almost at once.

Perhaps, after all, it was just my search that kept me from seeing the stranger who careened out of a slowly-passing crowd and jounced my father, who stepped back hand on hilt and froze, silent and attentive, awaiting word.

The stranger, his breath recovered, stood, an island as we were an island in the foot traffic, and said, "Pardon . . ." and no more. He was no tourist, but a new man to me and, apparently, to my father as well; he wore shining gray and his hand strayed to his own hilt and then left it. His eyes were cool, his face without expression.

"I ought to give you a lesson," my father said, still without moving, studying the other's face.

That man shrugged slightly, and offered his excuse: "I'm late—"

"You'd be later—if I had the time for you." And we strode on, my father in the lead for those few steps it required for me to match his pace. Even the simplest event, then, a collision in the streets, appeared to me to have a discernible and an important meaning, so that I looked back for the little man, and missed him when I could not spy him out among the crowds. But he had gone into some doorway or other, some trap or other; he was gone altogether, at any rate, we never saw him again, and he was, and remained, quite unimportant in any true sense. Yet he seemed somehow important; and, perhaps, if only to me, he was so. He served to advance the last challenge which I saw my father defeat, a small enough, a poor enough challenge, certainly, but one which I may remember now. And so, as example to me of my inattention, and stimulus to my memory of victory, he remains with me as do so many of the events of those days, for so many reasons, though quite probably they have no importance either for the keepers of this record, or the readers of it; yet it is my life with which you are involved, and the measure of importance must be in some wise my own measure. Of my life I can teach you of the Comity no more than the simplest portions; but all these portions, important to you or trivial, are equally alive, share equally in the life which, as they have given it to me, I have returned to them. And none can be ignored as easily as you might wish in your search solely for fact: what are facts, after all, against the living of them?

Frain, then—since you insist. Frain once more, the little angular man with the cold eyes that measured us both, in a big room more glittering than my father's which would one day be mine, sitting dwarfed behind a desk of true wood that kept us at a distance from the coldness he owned and the power to which he pretended (for we had more than Frain, it was an acknowledged fact that we were higher than his very dreams), all the showup panels of his Palace recessed and disguised within that room in the wooden framing of his walls—a senseless, a lavish expense with which we would have had nothing to do. Cash was never meant to waste on show, unless the glitter is spark to the game.

"Now the two of you are visiting me, is that it?" he asked us, for of course we had at once been shown to his room. And the bodyguards had left; in that room, no doubt armed and surrounded by arms, he had no fear of us. He seemed controlled and easy, no longer in the mood for headbreaking fight, but I felt still the anger he'd begun in me.

I let my father speak, as was his right. "You said something to the boy —" he began.

"I said something to Alex," Frain said now slowly. He had changed; he was far from urgent now, far from heated. He had changed, but we had no notion why. "I certainly did that," Frain went on coolly. "We had words, you might say."

I broke in to that smooth flow. "What did you mean?"

"I meant what I said," he told me without turning, for he still faced to my left, directly at my father's motionless figure. And my father now spoke before I had more chance to turn and own the conversation.

"You used a threat."

"I didn't mean to do that," Frain said, and it seemed to me the words were true. "I was angry."

But he was careless of result now. What had happened? My father said, "What was the threat? What's to threaten us?"

"You sound worried," Frain said, and his own sound was very nearly amusement, so that I fired up and shot heat back into that cool talk: "We're not worried. We demand—"

My father cut my childish words off directly. "We want to know," he put in, and Frain, ignoring me, spoke casually to him.

"You'll know. I promise you you'll know."

The words hung like a curtain between us, and I jerked at the curtain with words of my own: "We won't stand for—" but again my father made peace, made discussion, of my anger.

"We've come here to ask you."

This time a gleam was in Frain's eyes, and his head jerked back and forth between us; a hand grew restless on the smoothed, shining wood of the great desk. His words snapped insolence. "You'll stand for just what I want you to stand for. You had power here, once."

Father said, with perfect certainty and stunning calm, "We have power still, young sir."

But neither words nor tone halted Frain for more than an instant. "Do you?" he asked from his moving face, his restless hand. "In the next few days, you wonder about that."

My father moved forward a step and Frain's hands dropped below the desk, where we could not see them. "I've stopped my son's anger short," he said slowly. "I won't stop mine."

"And do you think your anger can hurt me?"

I began, moving forward: "I'll teach you what we can—" but my father restrained me with a hand at my shoulder.

"This is mine," he said. "Not a brawl for children, Alex, and not a learning-game." His hand moved me back and he stood before the desk.

"Are you not afraid of me?" Frain said in the tense language of the challenge, and my father, for answer, ducked across the desk, his hand brushing Frain's wrist as Frain came forward with his weapon, knocking the weapon itself to one side with a roar, and then using the same hand to reach forward for the bare throat of the little man . . .

But his strike had brushed the hilt and the weapon, at ready, had gone off; my father's hand stopped and he fell; there was noise remaining in the room and then there was silence while I stood, hearing nothing, seeing, as it seemed to me, nothing at all. Then there was Frain's voice, very small, very distant:

"Get him out of here. Just get him out." And after a time: "I didn't plan this. It doesn't matter, now . . . but I didn't plan for this."

And my father, lying across the great desk, a pool of blood at his shoulder, seeming at first to withdraw beyond breath, beyond life; my father, and my own motionless withdrawal.

And then, again, later, Frain's voice: "It's begun, now. It makes no difference when—a day or so—but now it's begun. I didn't plan for it now . . . but he won't mind. He's ready."

Of the man named Diamond we had not even heard.

A time without memory followed those moments.

And then my father was home, at rest, and awaiting.

The clock was ticking itself out. More and more softly now, the buzz of time circled and sounded in those massive ears and wove through that solid skull to echo within the body that breathed still, thought still, moved still, but now did no more than wait.

Time, that buzzing rope, was barely left him; and, for me, there seemed no more and no less than revenge. I did not in those first hours so much as think of the girl who was, also, my uncontrolled weakness. In that, at least, I was his proper son.

EIGHTH CALL

CHAPTER 15

But in the Wine-presses the Human grapes sing not, nor dance
They howl & writhe in shoals of torment; in fierce flames consuming,
In chains of iron & in dungeons circled with ceaseless fires.
In pits & dens & shades of death: in shapes of torment and woe.
The plates & screws & wracks & saws & cords & fires & cisterns
The cruel joys . . .

—from "Milton," by William Blake

HOWARD MOSSE

CHAPTER 16

I had the time to spend, and I had the money to spend (which is the most important thing there, you know) and the Reel looked like the place for me. I mean, I'd heard enough about it from other people, just as everybody does, I should think: there are always jokes about the man who lost his pants on the Reel and the woman who found her daughter, not mixed-company jokes, but I may as well be honest with you. And straightforward. I'm a businessman, no more than that, as you very well know from my tithe returns and other records of that sort, and I'd better stick to setting down a good clear story for you, not being some kind of free-living artist or, either, a playboy.

No, the Reel was my big moment, you see, the sort of fun I always imagined the rich people having, back where I came from; there was always some kind of pic in the day's info showing a man going off on vacation, or sometimes, for the matter of that, a woman or a couple, and a good many times the Reel was mentioned; what I mean to say is, when I did get there, at last, I could hardly believe it was me.

There, in the Way itself, once we were out of the pressurized sections and hunting our baggage idents and shipment-codes, all sorts of touts were scattered through the crowds, calling for one place or another, but the first thing I wanted was simply a hotel. I located a guide who told me his rooms were "the finest in the known universe," and went with him because, I suppose, he looked quite tall and handsome, a very well-set-up man; and the hotel itself, as things turned out, really was astonishing. There was a 3V right in my room, as there was, I understand, in every room as an ordinary service, and some of the other rooms even had tactile attachments; they could provide you with just about everything. I felt luxurious, just as I had expected to feel once I'd arrived.

I freshed myself up after the guide had left, and unpacked neatly, which is always a small pleasure, and then I decided to go out on the town and see what there was to see. My wife died three years ago, by the way, but I'm not at all sure in any case that Elma would have liked the Reel. Not her sort of thing, perhaps. But I kept seeing her, if you know what I mean, out of the corner of my eye all the time, as if she were asking me what I was doing there, Howard Mosse from Virgo, nothing special in the way of a man of influence, but just myself, there among all those luxurious things. Every street I saw was force-paved, by the way, and though you go everywhere on the Reel by foot or transport they have a special blink service from the ports. We'd come to the hotel by blink, my guide and I.

There was a restaurant right near the hotel, though it seemed to me it was run by different people; the decoration, at any rate, was soft and rich and quiet instead of bright and shining like the hotel lobby where the blink let us out. I walked in and the nearest free table lit, so I sat down there, and then a live waiter came over to me, walking as quiet-stepped as a machine might, and asked me what I wanted to have, and called me sir.

I was a little flustered, but I told him, nicely enough, that I wanted to see a menu. And he said, "Certainly, sir," and went away and got one for me. On Virgo we simply don't have that kind of service, nor want it, I suppose; and it made me just a little uncomfortable. But I have to admit that it is certainly luxurious, and just like the Reel, in fact.

I don't suppose I have to go into details about the food, or about any of what happened to me in the restaurant: that isn't what you're interested in, but you want me to go on to the gambling and what happened there, and I'll do that just as fast as I can. It only needs a little explanation first, so that you can understand it.

I think a man's time is his own, and he has no need to be ashamed whatever he does. I met some people in the hotel later that night, a couple named Frank and Abby Knollys from somewhere on Procyon (which they don't like called Prossy, of course, as I found out from them), and they were arguing right and left about the gambling places, so I said to myself, Howard, you'll have to see about that, if it's going to be as interesting as Frank makes it sound.

Because it was Frank Knollys who liked the gambling; his wife wanted to do the shops, that was all, though I think she may have had some private notions of her own. And at last Frank was bound and determined to go, and I asked him if I might come along, and he said he was glad of my company, to tell the truth, since it made him feel a little better among all the crowds of people who belonged on the Reel, and knew it. The two of us went out together one evening after supper. I'd spent some few days on the Reel by then, you see, and I felt like an old-timer, silly as people can be, and as if I knew what I was about.

We walked to the Palace, which was called the Prince, and we saw quite a lot on the way, though little of it was entirely novel to me by that night. We passed up the needle shop, since I'd rather get my own excitement from drinking, when I do drink (and Frank felt the same), instead of taking some injection you can't even taste or know much about until it has its effect on you (and then there's addiction, besides, and I'd seen a few people like that on the Reel and felt the danger of it and the expense), and then we went on by the girlie spots, which I didn't so much as look into because, to be frank, I felt as if Elma were right there with me, as if she were more real than the world I was on (because, after all, it's so luxurious and so fancy, there's so much entirely strange that you can't truly believe it, if you see what I mean)—at any rate, it was the gambling interested Frank, and we went right on until we reached the Prince.

That Palace was even larger and more shining than the hotel had been, as if they had all the space in the world to use and all the lights as well, and there was a friendly buzz of talk and movement as soon as we got into the entrance hall. And through that, at the far end, they took our hats and noted our ident pins, just two very cute live girls, teenagers, and gave us our blacklight marks, and we went right on into the main room. There was a crowd, it seemed to me, around every game, and there were games I hadn't even heard of.

Now, I was at one time a pretty fair player at poker, so I looked for a poker table right away, and found two of them, both round tables, in a corner of the place, so I headed for those. But Frank wanted me to try the shift game, and so the first thing I did was spend some time there. I suppose I'm just not quick enough physically to throw my weight just when the ball is at the right spot—as I say, poker's my game, or else a few doubles of wheel. Frank lost a little, too, but he says he's getting his eye back and any day he'll come and clean them out; I left him, after a time, to go on by himself, and headed for one of the poker tables. There was a triple-snake game that I stopped in front of, never having seen one before, with the channels all changing every second and the three balls coming down at different speeds, but it looked pretty tough to figure out. There were quite a few people playing its board, though.

I didn't see anything wrong with the poker game, but a man across the table from me, a big suntanned fellow only in his mid-thirties, tossed in his hand after one especially big pot and said, "You're not giving us guys a fair shake."

"What are you talking about?" the dealer said, almost as if he were bored with the answer. "Cleanest game in town."

The suntanned youngster only shrugged. "I was down by the Ball, and they run smoother there."

I asked, "What's the Ball?" not having heard of it, and meaning, of course, to find out as much about the Reel as I could: you know how that might be.

The dealer answered me, just as casually. "That's one of Yonge's joints, and you don't have to worry about him."

"What do you mean?" It sounded an odd thing to say, and I was still a bit curious.

"All I know is," the suntanned man said, "I liked the place."

"He won't last long," the dealer told him. "You listen to me: this is going to be the Diamond Planet before very long."

I said that it seemed to me the Reel was doing pretty well as it was, but the dealer told me, as if I ought to have known from the first, that he didn't mean that sort of diamond.

"At the Ball they play you square," the suntanned man said then, and got up to leave; and the game stopped until he was out of hearing.

"Just a sore loser," the dealer said as the cards went round and the action started up once more. "But he'll have to come back here before long."

"How do you mean?" I asked him. I picked up my hand and looked at it, and decided a small bet couldn't hurt matters.

"There won't be any Ball," he said.

Well, what with the talk and the glitter of lights off the roulette boards, and all the novelty, I was a little distracted and I didn't do too well during the evening; but I told myself that this was real excitement, glamour, like the mass-channel 3V stuffing, and it struck me that what the Reel actually was, was a true frontier planet, a historical oddity, the way things used to be at the edge before civilization was as solid as it now is; which gave me, frankly, the queer feeling that I was living some way out of my own time. Away back in the past.

But that, I know, isn't what you're interested in, how I felt and everything about that; and Elma always did say I talked too much for anybody's good but my own. I lost some at the poker tables, and later on when Frank was through for the night the two of us stopped into a Live Dream place to make ourselves feel a little more cheerful with the way things had gone, but I don't suppose you want to hear about that, either.

NINTH CALL

CHAPTER 17

PEER GYNT *(steps in the newcomers' path and, pointing at SOLVEIG, asks her father)*
Can I dance with your daughter?
THE FATHER *(quietly)*
You may; but first
We'll go in and pay our respects to the host.
(They enter the house.)

—from *Peer Gynt,* Act I, Scene iii,
by Henrik Ibsen, translated by
Rolf Fjelde.

ALEX YONGE

CHAPTER 18

Washed now, his wound having been dressed, and his eyes resting like fire with what might actually have been the pain itself of his hurt, my father waited for me. In the quiet of his own apartment (hidden, of course, behind recesses, in the maze beyond the offices which I have shown you), he lay in the state of his condition, served by a bodyguard hurriedly hired, closed by the rules of our headless household, but surrounded, still, endlessly and insistently, by papers and reports from our Palace; he had sent by messenger and beep a call for me, and, anxiously, I went up the stairs and round the many angles of our maze at what was almost a run, full of what I recognized as a new and even foolish fear, for it was fear not of the future but, somehow, of the past. I had not thought he would be hurt. It was the idea of his death which had been with me, an idea with which I had established relation; but now, in the fact of evening, even his wound seemed to me impossible of simple, unemotional acceptance. He had been the strength of that house.

"Well, Alex." The voice was the same as ever, though I had feared it changed; he was perhaps the same man. It was only that I knew more deeply than that, with a mind I could neither change nor control. When I closed the door and the bodyguard, seeing my father's signal, left us by his own route to wait closed out from our talk, his voice filled the room; but the room was not the same. "What do you think of me now?"

I stood at the foot of his bed, while he lay pillowed and half-smothered, as it seemed, with softness and rolling yards of care, and I stared at the big reddening face with a kind of young, perhaps excusable affection. "We've got to do something about—"

"Certainly we do." He waved one hand free of blanketing but the gesture was weak and he relaxed as if I had not seen it. "But that's not the point."

"You're hurt," I said, and added, because for the hearing of my own mind I had to add: "But you'll be better—"

Again, then, he cut me off with that weak gesture, and his voice, determined as it had ever been, expanded in the room. "I'll do what I must do. As we all do." It seemed to me that he smiled, but perhaps it was a trick of the overhead indirects; the light in that room, which was his and private, had always been troublesome to me. "But there is more for you to learn, and a short time to learn it in."

At that I cried out, "Father—" but he would not let me go on. His voice was as decisive as ever, which seemed to me both wrong and admirable.

"Let's have none of that," he told me with impatience, as if he saw me for even a younger child than I knew myself to be. "There's no time to spend in wind. But there are things to learn."

"I've followed you," I said in fright, for I had no wish at all to hear what was becoming, for me, a sort of testament, a sort of verbal epitaph for the man who lay before me: for my father. "I've learned—"

"You've learned the rules," he said, and there was no way to stop him: this was what he had decided, and this would be his action. He had, still, the strength of the house, and I had neither wish nor ability to go against him. He spoke evenly and slowly now, like a tutor. "But there are reasons behind the rules. There are always reasons, and they require a wise man to deal with them. You'd better be a wise man, Alex; matters aren't going to improve. Not yet, that's certain; and maybe not at all."

"What do you mean?" He had given me only words, words for further fear: there was nothing, as it seemed, for my learning in a rush of words.

He sighed, his hands shifted in the bed, he spoke again, lying back against the pillows as if to conserve strength. "You'll hear a lot of talk as you go on in the world, about what you've got to do," he said. "All the things you—as they say—must do, in order to—well, in order to keep yourself upright. Or principled. Or even strong. That sort of talk fills whole worlds, and here on the Reel there's an infection of nonsense. An infection that's growing every year."

"But it isn't nonsense," I said, as a pupil might speak. "Is it? After all, there are things which—"

"Things you have to do," he said. He tensed as if he lived the words he gave to me. "All right; but they're the obvious things. Keep a watch. Set a guard. Smooth out your fights when you can, win them when you can't, and win them any way that presents itself. Keep the glitter going—and never toss the glitter when a tourist is by, the glitter's what they live for, not the talk and not the truth. All that's obvious. But there's nothing else."

"Of course," I began, in wonder that what he had to say was so simple; it was not even a part of anyone's normal lessons: an infant knew as much, though until grown he might (as I had, often enough) forget.

"But you'll hear a lot of other things," he went on, as if I hadn't spoken at all, as if these words, these ideas, were a burden he had himself to lift from his body before he was interrupted. "You'll hear about law. Even here they talk about law—they chatter it."

"The tourists do," I said. "Unless you mean the natural laws of—"

"Not chance, and not mechanics," he said flatly. "The sort of law the tourists chatter. The sort they have to escape by coming here. There are some people on the Reel who think it would be a protection, that sort of law, if we had it."

"Protection?" The idea made no sense. Even the tourists spoke as if law were no good without enforcement, and that brought us back to our bodyguards. We had those: what more protection could this law offer us, if the law needed their protection as much as we did?

"Law's for the weak and the silly," my father said. "The notion is senseless. If you know what you're doing, you guide yourself, that's all. You guard yourself when need arises. In spite of the talk, in spite of the way things may look to you—you keep your position simple, keep it flexible. Let the other people worry about law. And let them worry about the things you ought to do."

It was a tourist's phrase. I repeated it. "Ought to do?"

"The rules of the world," he said. "There aren't any rules here except the obvious ones; and there shouldn't be. Rules are for the worried, and they make worriers out of the rest of us. As soon as you make a rule it's a burden to you, because you have to bother with keeping it. And wondering whether it makes sense in whatever new situation you're in—instead of acting sensibly in the situation without the junk of old rules to slow you up."

I thought I understood that much, and I told him so, quietly, respectfully, as one speaks to power.

"You don't understand," he said. He shook his head and tried to rise, but fell back again slowly, unwillingly; he spoke again while I kept silence and, fearful, watched him. "But you'll hear the talk, as I've heard it," he told me. "And worse than I've heard it, as well."

"Why—worse?"

His breath sighed out suddenly and his eyes shut; in a second he went on. "A man like Frain getting out of hand. In the old days . . ." He paused for a second, his eyes open now but not seeing me. "It's this talk about rule and law," he went on. "We didn't need it, then. We had trades, we practiced our trades. All of us, Palace people and workers, girlie joints, needle shops—what law could apply equally to us all? Why, our people came here originally to get away from law. To make a profit without that interference. We obeyed no laws but the ones we had to obey: the guide and the guard and the glitter." Now there was a long pause, and for the first time his voice seemed slightly to weaken. I held, for that second, all my breath. "But people grow afraid," he was saying. "And with fear comes law, and with law comes rule—the rule you can't overturn, because no one man is strong enough. And an association of men needs only more rule, more law. In that beginning fear—in that, a man like Frain sees his chance."

He stopped. After some seconds I asked him, quietly enough, "What chance? To make threats that he can't even—"

"No, not to make threats." Strength returned to his voice, as if in planning, in explanation, he drew somehow a kind of health. For that moment. "And not to wound me, either. But to take over; to rule. Or to have someone do it for him. That's what he aims for. That much is clear."

I could not, even if I had fact or theory on my side, dispute him. I asked only, "How can you know?" Later, only later, I was to marvel at the clarity of his sight into the new time.

"I watched him," my father said. "I saw his confidence. He has backing; he has strength."

"This—law?"

"Law gives no strength, Alex. As I've said. Law insures weakness. No,

Frain's assurance was of something bigger than himself. He's using fear now, using the fear that provides him opportunity. And it's up to you to see he doesn't get his chance, or doesn't hold it."

"I'll hold on—" I began, but he was too impatient with his own speech to hear me out.

"You'll hold on to what's yours; that, too, is a natural law. And it's enough. A natural law, a natural rule. No more."

"Father—"

"I know," he told me, hearing in my voice the change of tone. "You wish me well. No reason you should." He grimaced, seeing me still a child in his illness; as of course I was. "I owe you a debt for it; I'll pay it if I can. And if I happen to feel like paying it."

The words were one lesson more, but not a needed lesson; I knew the terms of reality, though the impress of a moment might suspend them for me; I was not yet grown, not yet fully aware. But I knew, and said, "Of course."

"Right," he said, pleased. "And now, get out."

"Father—"

"Get out," he said again. "I won't need you now. I wanted to talk, and you had to hear. The Palace, after all; it passes to you."

"Not yet," I said instantly.

"Perhaps not," he told me slowly. "But go."

"I—" What did I mean to offer him? Help was beyond me, beyond any but the skilled. And my wishes were no better than childish. They put a debt on him; they did no more.

"Now," he said.

And I left him, words spinning with the fear in my mind, words I have here set down for you, words which, perhaps, I am now beginning to understand and to see in their true qualities. For they were a mystery then.

So I went again downstairs, and watched the games, the brightnesses, the tourists laughing and crowding, the money and the power that was ours, the men we hired and the few we owned, all of the noise and the power. There seemed nowhere for me to go, nowhere for me to be myself, and at rest.

But there was one place; on all of Three there was, in the end, one place. When I set out it was fully dark.

And how can I make you see that passage, who may never have traveled our world? How can I show out for you the light of our darkness, the gleam and the pride of our power and our glitter? The Ways marked, the signs hung, all in order and all seeming to last a moment and forever; you have never seen the like, I cannot show you. Through that I walked, in expectation, and never saw it. You would have seen it; but the world was mine, I was careless of it. You could not have been careless: so we had planned it all.

I thought she would not have gone; because I hardly thought at all. But they had of course taken her already: she would not have stayed with Marge Sunday's special assignments, nor in fact with that place at all. The girl whom I saw when I asked there stared at me, clearly wondering, without words, what had brought me to such a search, a citizen of our city and our world asking, of all things on Three, for a new girl, a girl without specialties, a girl, even, without training—without, she said without words, all that she herself might find to offer me, to sell me for my satisfaction. But her words were polite enough, and she directed me well enough; next week, she must have reminded herself, I might be hers. Goodwill, we call it, and it's important on Three, as it must always be, sensibly, sanely, obviously, on any world; but I had never been so grateful for so common a thing.

She directed me to one of the training-homes, where the new girls lived and worked until they were ready for placement and prepared to begin earning their keep; training-homes of some sort were part of Marge's overhead, naturally enough, as training for the dealers and handlers was a part of ours. And as I walked away I felt her eyes on me, and her continuing curiosity, but I am not yet grown a full man, and so I cover myself with excuses for actions that would be shameful in a true man. A true citizen of our adult world.

Yet I still felt guilt; I'll be honest about that. And, walking down the ways of my world, I argued with myself about the guilt and came, as I had to come, to the determination that my action was childish and part of an untrue, a childish world; but my excuse still held, that I was not yet grown, and soon enough I stood before the doorway and saw my hand lifted to interrupt the beam; and an answer came quickly enough.

At first I was told only: "She's not ready for work; she's not meeting anybody yet," but I insisted, and the Yonge name carried some weight there, since Marge and my father were acquaintances and had traded favors now and again; I was led, at last, to a talking-chamber. I suppose that, by then, any wish of mine would have been acceded to: when Marge agreed she agreed altogether. But the talking-chamber was, then, all I wanted, all I felt I might request; which was more childishness.

She looked older somehow, as if a tight transparent mask were invisibly, inexplicably distorting her features, though yet she shone through distortion and was herself, seemed the person I had come to watch. She said at once, as the door shut behind her and we were alone, "Why did you come?" And her voice was different, more harsh and yet less certain.

"I wanted to see you. I had to see somebody." I was seated in a formchair, and she took another seat some distance away from me; there were chairs in the room closer to me than the one she chose. She seemed to relax into the foaming, but she did not altogether relax.

"There are all sorts of people here," she said, and her eyes shut and opened again. "Even in this one city."

"I didn't want to see all sorts of people," I said, and then, in an attempt to speak past the wall which seemed to have been pushed between us: "Do we have to argue?"

"I'm sorry," she said at once, and more warmly, perhaps. "But you can't know—you can't imagine—"

"Training?" I said; that, of course, as I thought, would be the trouble. "Lots of girls get the blues, until they begin to straighten out and—"

"You don't know," she said evenly. "It's not just—not what you think. Which would be bad enough. But it's not just that." I tried to remember that she was from Earth, and that she had childish ideas; but training would rid her of those. I hoped that a knowledge of the true world wouldn't be too much of a shock; it sometimes had a bad effect on new girls, girls who had to work their passage. But she was different, I told myself childishly enough: she was different.

So I was polite, I responded as if what she was discovering was new not only to her but to the world as well. "What do you mean?"

"Her—special girls." She said that much and sat silent, staring over my head at nothing I could imagine.

"That's good," I said, thinking of how a girl in such a business might truly feel. "It's better pay. It's—"

She broke out as if she, too, saw the wall and wanted to destroy it. "Can't we be ourselves?"

And she was right, of course. I said in recollection, "But those things were important—" and stopped: they were not important now.

"It's the world you live on," she said. "That makes them important. But—"

"Any world," I told her. "Any sensible world." For, from all I had heard, her world was not sensible: her world was for children, who believe in anything but the truth.

"No." She said that one word like the girl I had met, and became once again this new girl, this new creature. She was in training, and for some reason she suffered in it; I felt, once again, and more stupidly than before, a stab of guilt.

"I don't want to leave you here," I said. "You know that."

"Because you want me for yourself." The words were acid, twisted in her voice, and I thought for that second she was rejecting all idea of my wants, that she had other wants, of her own, so that I began:

"Yes—I need to—"

But matters were not so simple, not with this girl. "Profit," she said as if it were a monstrous idea. "It's all there is, isn't it?"

So she was learning truth, and the truth hurt her; she would recover, of course, but there was no salve for her then. I could only support the truth for her: "That's the way things are."

"They don't have to be," she said in a kind of resignation. "I wish I weren't—"

And again I thought I knew what she meant, and said: "I do, too."

"No," she said; in that one word, apparently, she could be herself. "Not what you think."

"I want you to be out of this, too," I said. "With me."

She shook her head; she very nearly smiled. "I wish I hadn't seen you," she said in a quiet tone. "Or talked to you."

I drew in a deep breath: the words, foolishly enough, actually hurt me. "I can—" I began, and then stopped and chose new words as I realized the truth; after all, it was part of the reason for my coming to her. "I could have bought you free. But everything is going wrong—"

"Diamond," she said as if the word were an explanation.

I stopped. I said: "What?"

"Diamond," she said, perfectly calmly. "I heard her talking about him. He wants—I don't know what he wants." I knew the woman she spoke of would be Marge Sunday; I had now to learn more.

"A *man* named Diamond?" I remembered what Frain had said, and it began to become sensible for me; and what my father had said as well. There was backing, I supposed.

But she had not heard me, caught in her own tangle of thoughts. "More, I suppose. He wants more. They all—you all want more."

And her words needed reply; she needed, still, explanation of the true world. "We have to go on—"

"She told me I was silly," she said, not as if she were speaking to me: as if she were alone, thinking aloud. "I didn't believe it then. What they did wouldn't stop me—never that. But you stopped me."

"Silly?" I asked her, searching for a clue to her self, her solitude. "About Diamond?"

"About—never mind." She seemed then to come back to me, to look at me across some imagined plain, too wide for crossing. Nearly too wide for speech. "Go away," she said suddenly. "Don't see me again. Please." The harshness, the uncertainty had come back to her voice.

I said what I meant to say, what I discovered in the saying of it was true; perhaps I had meant truly to say it on the night we had met. "I love you."

And she paused and looked at me, across that space, and at last said simply, herself, "No."

"I wanted to say it—" I began, but her words stopped me, held me. "I love you. It's all foolishness."

And that was true, and for me, then, meaningless: there seemed no answer but the words I put together for her. "I had to talk to you. That's all."

Her voice was harsh, distant, uncertain. "Not again," she said. "Please, not again."

"But if—" I don't know what I was then about to say. She never let me finish that thought for her. And so it was gone forever; there can be no return to it now.

"I can stand everything else," she said. "Without you. With you I couldn't—I couldn't be at all. Please."

And how, after all, was I to show her what I meant? What, after all, was I to offer her?

When I left she went back to her training without a glance into the room in which we had talked, without another word for me. What we had shared was gone: her walk told me that; everything that had happened between us belonged now only to the past, and perhaps not even to that any longer, as time spun by and we forgot. But I knew that could not be true; for me, I thought, it could never be true. Nor for her; but how was I to show her that?

What offer did I have to make? I could not even buy her free.

I wanted her out of the training; it was her only road to reality (and perhaps my road as well, in some way), but I wanted her out of it. I told myself, arguing as I went back, that she could go on until we had straightened Diamond and finished with all of that; surely it could not be too much for her. At any rate, she bore no visible marks; and they all complain of training.

Of course, we had both to grow up. Become adults. Learn the truth and live in it. As true for me as for her; and perhaps, after all, it was just that fact which mattered. Which stood between us.

TENTH CALL

CHAPTER 19

It would be well if the intelligent classes could forget the word sin and think less of being good. We learn how to behave as lawyers, soldiers, merchants or what not by being them. Life, not the parson, teaches conduct.

—from a letter to Channing Pollock
by Oliver Wendell Holmes, Jr.

MARGARET SUNDAY

CHAPTER 20

The gossip was getting around, which is always near the final stage of an event. For the ones involved in it, that is; for most of the world, most of the people who retail all that gossip because, frankly, there's nothing else for them to do and, for the moment, no other hole for them to fill in the world, it's nearer the first stage; but we won't worry about them: we haven't got the time and we haven't got the patience. Anyhow, I haven't, and who's telling this? Right.

Gossip, anyhow . . . the word was out on Diamond, and more than the word. From the way some people talked he had horns and a long red tail, and from the way others talked he had a halo. Which was of no interest to me: horns or halo, either they've got something to buy or something to sell, or Marge Sunday isn't in the same world with them. I'm a working girl, and there it is, start to finish, womb, as they used to say, to tomb. (Oh, I keep up on the old slang; deal with tourists and you will, too. Not that I wish it on you. Keep your dreams instead. Keep your fine altruistic dreams, don't bother me with them but by all means hang on to them for yourself. They're warm, and on some planets the seasons get pretty cold now and then.)

Anyhow . . . third start, and what am I avoiding? It wasn't only the word that was out. Diamond himself was out.

I saw him, right enough: he actually had the gall to come into my place and ask for me. I mean my headquarters place, where the best hang out. Just waltzed in as if he owned the place (my girls gave me the report, but I can trust my girls just as far as I can trust any headful of dreamstuff), and asked for me. By name. Personally. As if he'd been born right up top on the Reel.

Which, for all I know (now I come to think of it), maybe he had at that: he claimed it, I know that much, and there are stranger-cities over the waters, cities we don't have a lot of truck with, never having needed much from them. Nor them from us, I suppose. And a man like Diamond could have been born there, like as not; a man like Diamond could have been born anywhere. Or nowhere at all.

So why didn't he start with his own city? Sure: answer me that one.

Of course, you're not in the answering business. And I'm not in the question-asking business, either; what you want is the facts, which it's my business to provide for you, and my obligation as well, I imagine. And which I might as well get down to doing; what I'm beating around this particular bush for is more than I can imagine.

Well, he came in. My private office, where the furnishings are nice and fancy and calculated to awe the buyer or the seller out of 15 percent. Didn't do a thing to Diamond, not the glitter nor the glare. A slim gent, this one, a heavy mover but light with his eyes. A moustache, a little one, a bone tossed over his shoulder at vanity, but vanity didn't live in his looks or his clothes. Vanity was something else with this one, vanity was really pride maybe, but there wasn't any obvious weak point in him. I didn't find a thing. He sat down in a chair across my flossy, my fancy desk, and crossed his legs and relaxed, and looked at me as if he were wondering what I was visiting him for. The place was his, right?

Wrong. I waited a couple of seconds, just to let this character's gall set into the decorations of the room, and then I said, "Well? What is it you want with me?" I put my sharpest into it but I let him see no irritation. I'm a busy woman, get with it, I've heard it before and I've got six appointments to hear it again before closing, so unreel it, don't waste my time and maybe even yours. Like that.

But this one started from somewhere else. That was a trademark of his, that somewhere else. "I thought you'd be older," he said, nothing moving but his eyes and even his eyes doing nothing but running a catalogue of the place. Very nice, a lot like home, I may leave it the same when I own it tomorrow.

I stared at him. If you had skin, Diamond got under it—another trademark, now I come to think of it. "What do you mean, older?" I snapped back. "Look, I don't need any insults—"

"I say the first thing that comes into my head," he told me. Voice like a smooth, sharp wedge, he had no trouble stopping me. Not then. I suppose he meant it as an apology. "Now, how about this: it just entered my mind." He smiled at me. We're all friends together. My face said, Not me, buster, not so easy. Not me, shorthead. He went right on talking as if his face wasn't. "Must be tough running a chain of girlie shops."

"It isn't easy," I said. "I do all right. Except for visitors, of course. Those visitors do get you down."

"You don't have to get to gamma-radiating at me." His smile was very slow, very distant. I suppose it worked wonders with the right people. He gave it to me again and I handed it back frozen solid. That didn't set him back any, either. I tried again with words.

"I don't have to do anything, Mr. Diamond. I don't even have to listen to you. I haven't had much reason for it so far."

"You don't want reasons, do you?" He didn't turn a hair of that long head of his. He used the words and that was all. Only . . . then he looked at me and his expression was a little amused, as if he'd caught me being a kid. That got at me again, and I snapped back and handed him his ammunition.

"Look, who do you think you are?"

"I'm Diamond," he said. As if it were enough. As if it were always going to be enough. I don't tell people I'm Marge Sunday like that. And I think I could: I think I could get away with it.

He hadn't even bothered to think about it, one way or the other. "Congratulations," I said, keeping up my end of the battle, but it was an effort now. "And what does that have to do with—"

"I'm going to own the place," he told me, the same simple tone, the same relaxed character in my best guest chip of a chair, so it took me a second to hear him.

"You're—" Then it hit me, the thing he'd actually said. The thing he'd set up ripples in my air with. "What did you say?"

"I'm going to own the Reel," he told me, that relaxed man, that smiling man. "All of it."

I said the only thing that occurred to me to say. If I hadn't said it I might have started to believe him. "Listen, shorthead, what are you on?"

"I'm not on anything," he told me. Now he was amused again, all this foolishness of mine that had to be got rid of before he could get on to owning everything. "I don't have to be. Heard of the Yonge Palaces?"

"I've heard of them." Oh, believe me, I wasn't giving anything away to this Diamond. Answers to his questions, he could have those, but no more than the simplest of all the answers I found in my stock. Not that it mattered. He showed me just how little it mattered.

"Pals with the old man, aren't you? Grew up together. Made deals." Then he gave me his smile again: he knew, I didn't have to tell him. That's what the smile said this time, and I itched to have him cut to pieces. I swear I did. "But you don't have to talk about that," he added, rubbing it in. Oh, rubbing it in good.

"Listen," I said. I kept saying that word to this man. He shook me, he really shook me. "I think I'm going to throw you out."

"No, you're not, Marge." My name, and his calm, and he didn't move at all. He sat with his legs crossed, owning everything. I tell you, he had started to scare me. And you may have heard I don't scare with every fingersnap. By any manner of means. He just talked right on in that silk voice. That black silk voice. "You're the one who's going to listen," he said. "Because I've got you curious now, haven't I?"

It was the first wrong call he'd made. Curious wasn't the word that described me. It gave me a little fight back. "Don't try so hard," I said, almost bored with him or anyhow sounding that way. "We're all citizens together. Or are we?"

"Oh yes," he said just as gravely as if I'd wanted to know. "I was born here all right. You don't think some tourist could come up with this flash?"

"My tourists keep having flashes," I said. It was easy for a minute. "Adds to the overhead. And I don't know about yours. I don't even know what your idea is, not yet. We're only getting to that now."

"But I've told you," he said, so patiently I wanted to fry him over mild-hot plates. "I'm going to own the Reel."

"Sure," I said. "And I asked you what you were on. No weed's that strong. Where did you get the needle, buster?" I sat back and tried to stare him down, but he didn't stare down. That wasn't a game he played. He looked at me for a second or two and then he told me the rest of it.

"I said, the Yonge Palaces. They'll be mine in a few days. No palace owner is going to cooperate with me, Marge—not unless he's small enough or scared enough to buy out. And Yonge isn't either, so he has to be finished." He made a gesture with his left hand, throwing away Yonge. I watched his hand as if he had me hypnotized and he gave me another smile when he noticed it. "But people like you, Marge," he said. "I could make a deal with you."

I might have offered him anything. Women. Free deals. You name it and it was his. But if he'd been a tourist and nothing but a tourist he wouldn't have gotten to my door in the first place. If he'd been a tourist I could have worked on him. No, what he wanted wasn't tourist offers. He wanted what we all want, that's all: just that. Only he wanted more of it. And then more. I thought he was crazy, that's all.

That's what I told old Yonge when I saw him. But seeing him was a shock in itself. I'd heard of what had happened, in a vague sort of way, but the man looked truly old now. Shrunken, fallen in on himself, as if the juice had gone out of him when the wound had been made.

Lying in bed, there, alone. I came in and sat down in a chair and tried to pretend he wasn't dying before my eyes. It was bad pretense, but I had no time to adjust. I wondered how the son felt; I wondered, even, if he knew. They don't have to, the truly young ones; they don't have to know anything.

I was between his age and his son's, of course, but always closer to the old man. Seeing him was a little like seeing prophecy. Someday, some turn of the world, and I'd be like that, and my profits gone for nothing.

Or gone only to make the passage easier, the long one, womb to tomb. Which is all there is, all anything is for. He disturbed me, the old man.

"Diamond?" he said when I'd told him most of what I had to tell. "That's what Frain talked of. A Diamond world. But we couldn't know he meant a person." His voice was old, too, and tired, coming across the room a breath at a time. His hands moved a little on the bedclothes as if he wanted to do something, but there was nothing for him to do anymore.

"He's mad."

But old Yonge said, "No," and stopped and breathed, and then said, "He's as sane as any of us. He wants the same things. Only he's not going to get them. Not from me." Then he stopped and breathed again, slowly, and said in almost an idle, a careless tone, "I wonder where he came from."

"Off-world, maybe," I said, in spite of what Diamond had told me. Because of what he'd told me, it could be: here, alone in this room, to get back at him somehow. But the dying man wouldn't let me.

"Never."

"Anyhow—"

"There'll be work to do," he said suddenly. "If I can get my son to do it." And then, with a lapse into weakness: "He's a good boy."

I asked myself for one second if I had to tell him, but of course I did: he was still planning, still active, and, it might be, better at it than I have ever been. He needed to know everything. "He's gone asking after one of my girls. Special crews." I watched the old face: he grimaced, once, no more.

"He hasn't that sort of trouble."

"She's new," I said. "They met once."

He nodded, thinking that out. A good mind, a fine mind. We'd been through some deals, here and there, in and out. I waited the way I always waited. In the end he said, "I'll take care of it."

"Sure." There was no room for sentiment, no room to let the boy grow out of such things naturally. Everything had to be rushed, now, and the boy grown before we were into our battle. Before we were engaged with Diamond.

"Did he say anything?" the old man asked me. "Anything definite?"

"He made me an offer."

"Take it, Marge?" The eyes shone at me for a second and he grinned. One spark of life: it warmed the room. It was enough.

"Now you're the mad one." I gave him back the banter, as we always had, but he went serious on me. Dying, careful, slow.

"Maybe you'd be mad not to take it, Marge. Maybe he'll win."

"He can't win," I said. "If he wins, we're finished."

His head shook back and forth on the pillow, saying no. "If he wins, the Reel is finished."

"Same thing," I said, and he didn't disagree with me. He was weak and growing weaker; he began to speak and then seemed to forget the words; for a long time I sat and waited.

"But how are we going to stop him?" he asked me in the end. There was only one thing for me to say, and it had to be the right thing to say. It had to be the right answer; he was better than I, or he had been; but now he was asking me.

"We'll fight," I told the wounded man, and got up, and walked over to the bed, and grinned down at him, just as good a grin as ever I gave a soul. "We'll fight."

ELEVENTH CALL

CHAPTER 21

I love and I hate.
I don't know how this happens.
It happens. It hurts.

—by Catullus, translated by
Laurence M. Janifer

ALEX YONGE

CHAPTER 22

It was over, she had told me; and she had done that telling with every word and every gesture she owned. There was no mistake about that, none at all. But I couldn't convince myself that she truly believed what she'd said so completely; not she, not Christie. We'd somehow already been too much to each other for a conclusion that quick and that easy: we'd become too important to each other. In any case, that was the way I felt, and maybe the way I had to feel, being as childish as then I was, and I'll agree to a verdict like that without any argument at all. Because (you see) it doesn't truly make any difference. The childishness of the matter, in fact, had no effect on me whatever: I knew it, all right, and I could hardly help but know it; but I ignored it, and as far as I was concerned it had come up in my thoughts, been dismissed and was gone. Telling me I was childish didn't accomplish anything, not then, even when I was the one doing my own telling.

I had to see her. What I felt and thought was, in the end, as simple as that: I knew that one fact, and it seemed to be all I did know. I had to make matters between us right once more—whatever "right" may have meant, whatever outworld romance I was involved in. And if I'm harsh about it now, when I recall it and spin it out for you, depend on it that

I'm not as harsh as I ought to be, considering—taking into account the way we live here, and the actual world we live in: we haven't got time, here on Three, for any of the usual dream nonsense. That's what we sell, and no sensible man will buy it; but I wasn't exactly sensible at the time.

My dreams prove that, if nothing else does: they were wild and dizzying flashes that night, full of the old times I had never known, full of faces and figures who were not myself and not anything I knew, full of words of power and command, all the words, all the truth and the lie, of our world; they were bad, and they seemed to have no end, but to revolve forever in a sparkling, disconnected circle around me; I remember I came awake shivering and fell back to a further dream and a deeper one, brighter, a mass of puzzles without connection thrown into that endless circle; and, at last, morning came and I stood up out of the warm bed and felt the cold of wakefulness on me with a sort of relief. But the one idea I'd had was still with me, and that one idea drove me out as quickly as I could move, so that I hardly even stopped with my father, but only found out what the doctors called his "condition": they went on calling him "unchanged," as if it were the only other word they knew, using it as though it were some sort of magic plaster of wind, saying it even though he was visibly weaker, visibly thinner, though he seemed even to have passed through years of aging in that one night; I suppose they were frightened, too, as I might have been if I'd had room to be, at the thought of some real weakness coming to the head of our Palace. And the image of my father, pale and faraway, stayed with me as I went, though I had no time for anything but the image: I had time only for Christie. I thought only of her.

Oh, it was silly enough, childish enough; but I thought of her by her own name. She had become, for me, no tourist but a true person, not merely a need but entirely and absolutely a person in her own right. My world, in fact, had shrunk to that one name, to that one object, and so the object became enlarged; I could not help myself, but that should never have occurred.

And so I arrived at Marge Sunday's main studio, where I thought I might get some information on where they'd taken her and how I might see her. But there was no information for me there; the girls I saw made that plain enough.

I could not discover, not for certain, whether they were telling me the truth when they said she would not see me, or whether they were simply handing me off with some tourist tale, something useful in getting rid of me and no more than that. But they repeated their single story, and I got progressively louder; I set up a racket, in fact.

And the racket got me nowhere at all. Marge's girls were accustomed to that sort of fuss: there were always tourists who got the wrong idea, of course, or who fell harder than usual for one of the girls. I was stonewalled, no entry and no retreat. So I did the only thing there was left for me to do: I stuck, and I made my racket.

Eventually, of course, Marge herself came out to see me. I'd banked on that: she wanted no more crossing with my father than she might have to accept in the normal way of business. Naturally, I rated no interview with Marge on my own: I was trouble and bother, and she knew it, and I owned nothing worth her exchanging time for it. But, for my father or myself, she came out, and dismissed the girls. When they were gone she looked at me on her doorstep and said, "All right."

I said, "Inside," and she nodded, and we went through a glittered hall while the door swung shut dead-silent behind us, and then round a corner and past three or four rooms that made most fanciness look dustbrushed: Marge did herself well in display, as she had to do. At the end of that passage she opened a plain door and we went into her private rooms, which were more of the same. No need to describe the shine off the furnishings or the solid light curve of the walls; she sat behind her desk and I dropped into a formchair and she gave one brief sigh and shut her eyes.

A second went by and she opened them, a hard woman and a good one in her trade. "Well, young Alex," she said as flatly as I'd ever heard her, "what's all this about?"

She called me young, of course, to put me off my balance, but I wasn't young enough for that gaff. It irritated me, no more, and I said in a voice carefully as flat as her own, "You've a girl. I want to see her."

"Always ignoring the rules of my place," she said casually, "I understand she doesn't want to see you."

"Let me hear it from her." This was fencing, this was the joined battle we learned to wage, on our world. A good way to live, a satisfactory way, true and adult.

"And then," Marge Sunday said, "there are the rules. Which don't snap open for every five-minim request, as you ought to know." She paused and sighed again and I'd have sworn she was genuine about it. "Now, really, Alex," she went on when she noticed I'd taken time to think out a move, "do you have to dramatize this? You know perfectly well—"

Her words gave me the opening to force through. "I know perfectly well that I want to see her."

She only smiled at me, seeming remote and controlled; she was very expert, as of course she had to be. "And, like a child," she said, "you think that what you want commands the world."

"I only think—"

"A tourist dreams that way," she said, and her words had force; she leaned forward across the desk and I saw with surprise that she was not fencing; that she meant, in fact, exactly what she said and the manner in which she said her speech. Distantly, I even felt a slight pleasure that she treated me so as an equal. "A tourist thinks he can wish and make the world come true, his world, the world inside his own inaccurate head. And he can—and it does. For a price. Because we arrange it for him. But this is no game, Alex; this is no Dream Line. This is the Reel."

I left her a space of silence after that, and then said all there was left for me to say. "It can be arranged." And she countered it, of course, as I knew she would:

"But why should it be?"

Outside the soundproofed glitter of that room, there was a dim noise which continued. I paid it no mind, but Marge looked up for a second, her attention divided, and I made my plea:

"Because I ask it. I haven't asked that many favors."

Marge's gaze came back to me slowly. "You're trading on your father's credit," she said, and for that weak reply I had a new attack.

"Am I?"

"He's still your father," she said. "In spite of what's happened. And he's still in control of—"

"Is he?"

And I had shaken her: so much was visible. Perhaps, in another second, I might have won my point. But we had no time remaining, for the noise outside was louder, and Marge's head went up again, waiting; in that second the noise grew, and then a voice outside shouted her name: *"Marge!"* loud enough to be heard through the soundproofing. Marge Sunday stood up, all in one motion, as if I weren't there at all.

"What's going on?" I said. But she shook her head, no more, and went to the door and jerked it open. Shouts, crashes, an incredible volume of sound washed through into the room like a wave of actual water; we were frozen by it until a girl flew by, her clothing ragged and herself in rushing disarray; she saw the open door and gasped a few words as she went on toward the front of the place:

"Marge, come on—it's happened—"

Marge Sunday took one second to turn back to me. "Get out. There's no time." Then she was out the door. I followed her quickly, into the screaming noise. But it was nothing but noise for a second; the people causing it were round the corner, in the first corridor.

We came to them. There were four of them, men in black tightfits, crushing what they could and smashing the place as well as the girls who were mixed with them, six or seven of Marge's girls. They know what to do in a fight; they have to, of course. But they weren't doing well: the men were armed with stabs and beamers, and the girls hadn't had time to hunt up anything of that sort.

Hangings went, the glitter fell and piled, somewhere glass shivered with a high, grinding crash, and the girls screamed over it all, not words but sounds, the men only panting with their fight: they seemed all strong enough for bodyguards, as I guessed they were, but they were strange to me; which meant little enough. There was no time for thought. Marge Sunday didn't even notice I was there; she had time only for the battle, and she went into it as if she had planned every move days before. Her arm swung and a man went down, but she was pinned by the crushing of bodyguards and girls in that narrow corridor and could not break fully free; and I stayed back, frozen for that second. This was not my fight, nor a fight I understood.

I remember, now, a few single seconds, disconnected like pieces of a dream: one of the girls shouting and trying to run forward against the crush and butt a bodyguard, being caught up and shoved aside by some mindless motion of the fight as a bracket of lights sagged and moaned and then fell at her side with a pop as it went to powder; another girl held by the waist and swung up at the edge of the crowd, kicking and screaming thinly as she tried to break free while the bodyguard who held her laughed, waited and then tossed her toward the center crush: she disappeared and he was caught by Marge Sunday's swinging fist, but he slid aside from it and returned to the fight.

I remember that, and the wreckage. The rooms we'd passed were a tumbled collection of glass and glitter and fractured wood; there were broken mirrors in pointed great bits, and the remains of chairs in shreds and bones; the walls were scored and dulled, the lights half powder on the floors, one door dented and hanging aslant . . .

They broke suddenly, the four bodyguards, together in a pack, and ran for the door; two girls screamed and stepped toward them and the four turned again and showed their beamers. The girls were still, and for one absolute second of suspension there was a dead and waiting silence in those corridors.

The four men were at the door, which swung loosely open. One of them yelled out a single sentence in a hoarse, scratched voice: "So you'll know—this is from Diamond." And they scattered, beyond chase or snare, gone like last year's leaves.

Gone.

No one, it seemed, wanted to move at all. I heard Marge Sunday say the one word over again to herself, that was all: only the one word, as if it were all she could think, or the only savage comment she could make on what had happened.

"Diamond."

TWELFTH CALL

CHAPTER 23

It is a metaphysical doctrine that from the same antecedents follow the same consequences. No one can gainsay this. But it is not of much use in a world like this, in which the same antecedents never again concur, and nothing ever happens twice.

—Sir James Clerk-Maxwell

X

CHAPTER 24

Anytime now, maybe yesterday, when the light cracks and fills the streets up, when the dark good night comes on and down, anytime at all the right time is here; my name is not anymore, not any difference, why should you bother to, bother to, bother to, only sometimes there is a time with not enough in it, not enough, and that's all the time I mind, that sometimes, you know it, when the light won't go away, when the crash comes down like all the light in all the worlds. Because it can't until the end, a voice in one time said that, said until the end, and something still hears it (maybe it's me) and the light comes on and comes down and all, entire, everything and inside all the skin, all fills up with the light and that hurts, you know it, that burns like fire burning through on some old day. But there is not any fire anymore, either, and there is very little more of anything except sometimes not enough; there is sometimes a not enough time, and no getting rid of that, believe it, no filing that down or filling that up, none at all, because they slap out a price to you and the price is the thing, you got to have the price or else and until, I don't know who that was anymore, but I won't tell. Because if I did I would have to, you know it, you can see that much. In the good dark.

It's a city, I have that much left I know it's a city, and in the long dark

I walk and look and there is a place I am but it is not dark now anymore, never, with the lights on when the star goes down; that is a star, in the daylight, what they call daylight here but their day is their time and not mine; maybe I am not one of them and maybe I am, that becomes hard to tell. Only today there is enough for today and maybe while you waited and asked me to talk and tell, spiel and spill, pop and chop until, until, until, maybe, in that time, time has gone circling by with the sound it makes like a man saying long ago until the end, until the end, a soft and whispering wellbottom sound, and I can remember, I can remember everything and spin it all out for you in this fine place, here, now, where darkness is and nothing hurts because there is not any ever crash here, is there? And time does not ever matter anymore, or the face and the voice; and maybe it didn't, any day now it won't, maybe yesterday. How did I come here?

There was once when I used to be somewhere else and they said to me when I was down a kind of help that was a way up, here's a way up, they said that, and so it was there for me and then more of a way than that, and in the end here I was, where they sell you anything, anything, anything at all but you have to get the price they slap out, and the price goes up all the time, at first there was enough all the times and enough for a payment to come here, all myself, a ship in the long time, in the long space where it is always the good dark but I left that and came here where the light shines and crashes through the skin because in the light you can get more of what you need, there is a sign I have to look at, open my eyes and look for it, says what it says and there is my place. Now. Because at home there are uniforms, always uniforms and the hard voice and then never anymore, but there are no uniforms for me here, no person to look for me here. For the sign that says my white, my powder, my needing every day to take away the light now, take away the crash now so there is nothing more to hurt. She knew that. She knew that.

But she wanted me to keep my name (and this is away in some other time somewhere in some other world), she wanted me to keep in the filthy light where they run with iron claws and fire through the open skin, she wanted me to do whatever that was I don't talk about that and I said, I said, I said, I would not come back, I would stay here until the end and she didn't care; that is true, that she didn't care, not enough, because I showed it to her, a heap, a pile, a white powder more than my money had for me and said it was for her, said that, because she was mine and she had followed me and found me but she would not take the powder, would not come with me there and then because she did not care enough and she went away. Until the end. That was in some other time, you know it, that was a long time gone whatever that is, and now sometimes the light is not too bad because I have to make my money the best I can imagine to make my money, because they have a price here, and they give me money sometimes, that's true, sometimes, but only strangers do that, only strangers who come here and leave again, until the end, she gave me money when she left and that was all but that was enough, the money bought me darkness through a circle of time, a long spinning circle of time I forget, where there is no light anymore, I forget all of this and I won't tell you about it, no. I was somewhere else and there were uniforms, there was a law and their big hands to stop me but there is no law here just take what you want, and pay for what you want, what you need, so the money was all she could give me, because she did not care enough, she did not. Oh, she went away, you know it, she did not care until the end but the light is coming back now, coming on and down through the skin and somewhere the voice is coming too and the face and the crash is coming: I know what that crash is. You give it to me, this once, you give it to me, money, what I need, this once and never again, never again because she didn't forget, only I forgot and I forgot, and there is not much time now anymore, not much time in time to leave, to go, to find, to stop. There is not much. But this once to pass me through the light that never stops anywhere to the good dark and back where she waits because she gave me money and her face was tears in all her face when I saw it that is back now, and I can stop her being like that, I can change her, change the face and the voice, change it all, really I can do that, and you would like me to do that because anyone would if you saw the face and the tears, it must be done, stop her from crying when she leaves, she always cries when she leaves every time I think of it but this is the last, the last, the last until the end and until because there is still time. Please: because.

Hurts. And so must become a time and a light and stop. Until anywhere, anytime, I have said it, enough for now, told and told what you wanted told, later anything, anything at all, you know it, sure, anything only stop her crying stop the tears until the end. Stop the light. Stop the light. Stop the light.

THIRTEENTH CALL

CHAPTER 25

LUCIFER: How, Faustus, how dost thou like this?
FAUSTUS: O, this feeds my soul!
LUCIFER: Tut, Faustus, in hell is all manner of delight.
FAUSTUS: O that I might see hell and return again,
how happy were I then!

—from *The Tragedy of Doctor Faustus,*
by Christopher Marlowe, Scene VI

ALEX YONGE

CHAPTER 26

That frozen second passed and, as everybody seemed to move at once, I got one of the girls by the arm, hardly feeling the contact, knowing only that she was what I needed: my whole sudden plan was in my mind as if it had been put there by someone else. The girl whirled at me and made a sound that wasn't a word, in fright; the others were still reacting, though the men had gone seconds before, and only Marge Sunday was trying at once to establish some sort of order. I didn't bother with any of that. I said, "Where is she?" and the girl stared at me.

"She? Who—"

"Christie," I said. "She's got something to do with this, we have to find her, at once—" I went on, using words only to maintain the sense of urgency in her, words that wouldn't have had the slightest chance of convincing her of anything at all under normal circumstances. But these weren't normal circumstances, and the tone was more important than the words I used: she was frightened and had no time to think, and I had only one subject, still only one subject, on my own mind.

She was caught, of course, and before she thought at all gave me an address in the older part of town, near the original settlement hotels at the center; I needed no more; I said, "Good," and left her there in the whirl of destruction and confusion. Marge Sunday was shouting something to them then, and they were beginning to come back to themselves; I suppose that was fairly fast, but she'd have girls like that, and training like that. I knew now where Christie was and what she was doing, and now that Diamond was active, now that he had at last made his deliberated move, so much more reason existed for me to find Christie, to protect her, to keep her, in fact, all to myself while my father and I somehow invented between us some beautiful, iron-bound scheme to keep Diamond at bay and destroy him at our leisure . . .

This was not an adult reaction, not anything resembling a sane process of thought, and of course I knew that quite well; but what difference did it make to me? Now that I had the address, now that I was in motion, what difference did anything beyond that motion make to me?

Outside, the place seemed oddly peaceful after what we had seen and fought: I wandered past tourists who continued simply to peer and pry, poke and wonder, full of hope and full of cash, full of wants we were all willing to salve, needs and wounds we were prepared to accept and service, all as if nothing whatever had happened; the constant and continuing flow went on the way time goes on, tick after tick, every minute the same no matter what happens in it, or doesn't happen. What Diamond had done, and might still do, what, in short, Diamond truly and simply meant, existed so far behind the scenes, for them, as to be invisible, limited only to us who actually lived on Three, who knew the truth not only of our world but of any: it was, after all, the truth in which we were so happy to deal. There were the caught and the curious of all types, from the merest peerer to the addicts in the needle-shops, but for the addicts no conceivable change could make a difference: they were even further from the true, the adult world than the normal usual tourist: nothing, anymore, could touch those cold, distant dreams away from the light. And so I was surrounded by what seemed to me, suddenly and without reason, an oddity: human beings who knew nothing of our battle with Diamond—or, in fact, of mine, either, with Marge Sunday and now, as I could see plainly enough, with Christie herself.

I knew, as I've said, what I was entering before I reached the place, through circles of crowded streets push-full with the packs; that address, in that section, was one I'd heard before, one we had all heard before, very popular with certain grim soft tourists. I suppose everyone had noticed what I had begun to see, that whole worlds seemed to center themselves round one form or another of release, one type or another of promise or itch or gaff: gambling, sex, the Dream Line or places like this one. It was, for those who wanted it, one of our very special attractions, one of the items which perhaps no other world within the Comity could offer, very simply and thoroughly provided for the ones who had the need, or the curiosity; and there are more of those than you might think. Makes you wonder, sometimes—if you're built to wonder.

I opened the big wooden doors and stepped through into the gloom within, and one of Marge's girls spotted me right away, a hostess who was good at her job. Of course she hadn't had any word from Marge about me, and she didn't know me: girls in that place wouldn't, since their show was very strictly for tourists, who had frustrations to work off —which is what made them tourists, if you see what I mean. This one was dressed in black slick leather, all formfit or made to look it, and she crossed the big entrance hall toward me smartly and quickly, saying, when she'd reached me, "Yes, sir?" in a voice as soft as cloud and as hard and distant as Marge Sunday herself.

Well trained. I said, my plan still in my mind and all of it working out as I'd hoped, "I'm looking for Christie Chesson."

"Chesson's not ready for—" she began, and then stopped and seemed almost to change personalities. In a voice more normal, less soft and less hard, she said, "Hey," and looked at me; for the first time, truly looked at me. "How do you know about her?" she asked me. The edge of suspicion was in her voice, but it was only an edge; there were explanations, after all. "She isn't ready at all yet."

"I'm not a tourist," I said flatly, and waited for her to make the next move: she said one word.

"You're—"

I cut her off like a man with business on his mind and no time for converse. "I'm looking for Christie Chesson," I said, just as flatly. "Marge sent me over." That would do for an explanation; the rest of it she could feed herself. I looked the part, tight and tough like a messenger or a bodyguard.

No more than a second passed, a single eyeblink while she thought the situation over. Then she said, "Sure. Where? You taking her someplace?"

It was almost too good to be true—as the tourists would say. It was what I'd planned for, and the plan had worked; I felt all right, but not surprised. The thought of talking to Christie washed over me, but I crammed the feeling down: she was going to need argument, and I had to have a clear head. There seemed no room for sentiment, no room for emotion; whatever had kicked me into the situation, the situation was a part of real life, and wanted clarity and sense.

"I'll see her in an outside hall," I said. "Not in one of the cells. Private, though—I'll be taking her off, maybe, but I've got to ask a few questions first."

She nodded slowly. "Sure," she told me. "All okay. Want to wait in Reception until I find her?"

"Okay." She led the way round the curve of the entrance hall to the big door, opened it for me and held it, and I went through. There was no glitter here, naturally, just pale, dull lights, a shine of metal; the entrance hall was almost in darkness compared to other sorts of places, certainly compared to our blazing Palace. Trust Marge Sunday to dress her shows right; this, I supposed, was what these particular tourists were going to want, and to expect.

Privacy was the watchword here, privacy and secrecy; I could see, when I thought about it, how that would be important to the customers.

And when I looked around Reception, after the girl had gone, the door had shut and I was alone in silence, I saw more good dressing. The room was big and vaulted, dark and mysterious, with pictures illuminated by faked candle-bunches on the dark wooden walls, and no sound-effects at all. Some of the pictures were old engravings, or copies of them, blown up four and five times normal size, some were live shots or even tridis, posed, of course, and then retouched for effect.

All of them were scenes of torture. And Marge Sunday knew her business: they were well made, convincing, and, I supposed, exciting to the tourists who wanted that kind of thing. And there were a lot of tourists like that.

They need to work off frustration, I imagine, or hate or revenge or something of that sort. Whatever their home world gives them, it isn't enough of the right stuff, and the feel of that missing piece, whatever it is, backs up on them until they have to blow off somewhere, and need a violent way of doing it. As I say, if you like to wonder about that kind of thing, it was a good place to start you wondering; all I know about it is this: that anything is for sale on Three. Anything at all.

The girls there made a good living, I'd heard, and the cash and tips were better than in a straight house. And of course they weren't truly hurt, not badly: padding and charge fields took care of that for them, easily enough. All the same, there were a few girls who didn't like the life, or couldn't see the profit in it for themselves; but they were mostly like

Christie, when I came to think about it: outsiders. Any girl from Three could see the sense in that place, and the profit built to come out of it.

I waited, until the pictures got dull and there wasn't anything left to think about; I'm not basically a wondering type. No tourists came in to break up the wait; the place did, as I'd heard, what was mostly a darkside business, after the sun curved out; shadows helped the tourists get in the mood, I suppose. There was some trade in the daylight hours, sure, but a half-hour or so without a tourist wasn't too much of a surprise. After all that time, I was sitting in a big high-backed chair of some black wood, not thinking about anything in particular, and the door opened.

My head came up and I saw her, all alone. She'd come a step or so into the room and the door shut behind her before she could change her mind, but she stood still, not looking round at it. I'd never seen anybody stand so very still. She said, "You."

"It's me," I said, my voice still flat, but with a new tone in it I couldn't help putting there. "I came to see you."

"Give up," she said. "Go away." She didn't move, she hardly seemed to breathe. She stood staring at me and I couldn't tell at all what she was thinking. It wasn't a pleasant minute.

"I came to—"

"There's no profit in this for you," she said, and her voice had an edge to it now, a distant edge that wasn't quite irony or even scorn, but maybe a sort of regret aimed as much at herself as at me. "That's what you care about, isn't it? That's what you know?" She took a breath, and I didn't say anything, and she spat out the word as if it were an obscenity for her: "Profit." Her head turned for the first time, toward the door, and then back again to me. "I hear them talking here—"

"I came to take you away." That finished what I'd started to say before she had begun her speech; I said it, and found nothing to add to it.

"To be with you," she said with that same distant, edged regret. "To be the same as I am here—"

"Not the same at all," I said, but she shook her head: in that stillness, every motion she made seemed to be emphasized, brightly lit, truly important. She said, flatly and with no doubt in her tone:

"The same."

I drew a breath. My plan was gone now, the immense, careful structure of argument and logic had gone when I saw her, and I could only speak what I thought: what, in spite of my own restraints, I felt. "Christie, please believe me—"

"How can I believe you?" she asked me with a sudden heat. "How can I even see you—here?" She looked now around the room, at the glowing frames of the pictures, at the scenes they showed, as if they were scenes from her own training, as they might have been; she had no liking for the place or for her position there, but of course she was an outsider and couldn't be expected truly to understand. "I don't want to think about you anymore," she said, and then, as if the words had burst out of her: "It hurts me—does that make you happy? It hurts me. The way they want to hurt me here—"

It was as if I used words, sounds, as a true salve for her wounds, for her pain and her trouble: "Christie, Christie—" There seemed no other words for me to use, no other thing for me to do. And then I stood up and went to her, my hands on her shoulder so that her warmth and her fright flowed through into my skin, and we stood together, just in that way, for a second or so. She didn't move at all, and when she spoke her voice was very low, as if she recognized, in spite of her words, defeat.

"Let me go. Please." Another second passed and she said, "Alex, let me go."

But she had used my name, and that was perhaps some sort of spell or signal between us of which even we could not fully be aware. I held her without moving. "I want you to come with me," I said slowly. "Escape this place." For if she disliked the place and her job, I would use that: I would have used in building her conviction any desire at all.

She breathed out, making a small sound like a sigh. "I can't stand it here," she told me, as if she no longer had choice or volition regarding her words and tones.

"Then come," I said instantly. "Now."

"But—"

She had weakened; she was mine. "I'll work everything out," I told her, and my hands tightened very slightly on her shoulders; I saw her eyes waver and decision finally, entirely, leave them; she was mine. "Come," I said.

"Alex, you'll have to be—"

"Whatever you want."

She took my hand, raising her own to her shoulder. I gripped the hand hard, let go of her other shoulder and turned toward the big wooden door of that room.

Marge Sunday was standing, very quietly, in the doorway.

FOURTEENTH CALL

CHAPTER 27

If others had not been foolish, we should be so.
The soul of sweet delight, can never be defil'd.

—from "The Marriage of Heaven and Hell,"
by William Blake

MARGARET SUNDAY

CHAPTER 28

It was nearly ten minutes after he'd gone that it occurred to me to ask about him. Blame that on the excitement, if you have to blame it on something. Diamond had made his move, and Diamond took precedence over anything else. He had to, of course: it was clear enough that Diamond was not about to settle for anything much less than the Reel, wrapped like a present and dropped in his hand.

But when the Yonge kid did come to me again, it wasn't too hard to figure out what had happened.

That, I told myself, was all I needed, some flower-struck boob, some romance nut, creating more complications for me, and for everybody. As if, with Diamond around, I didn't have enough to worry about. With Diamond on my neck, and on everybody's neck. I stopped whatever I was doing at that second, scraping away the mess, probably, and looked around.

Well, the place was straightening, slowly. I'd sent out a beam for some repair work, and the crawlers were floating in, clanking a little, and beginning to set to work on the place. The girls had been in a state, naturally, but I calmed them down a little, stacked them happy and peaceful in the private rooms and put out a NO ADMITTANCE sign for an hour or so. Then I set out.

I was steaming angry by that time, trailing clouds of it. Not that the Chesson girl was important to me: one girl isn't going to make or break an operation this size. If that were all my worries, I could have let her go without a spasm. But an organization doesn't allow the rules to bend like that. You've got to run it tight or not at all; the girl was in, and she stayed in. Or how did I know somebody else wouldn't scat out the next day? One girl makes no difference, but a hundred girls taken one at a time can stir up trouble for me, and make more vacancies than I have an easy way of filling. All it takes to start a scat like that is the first one. And Christie was not going to be it.

I opened the door just as he was persuading her to get out. Though it didn't seem to me she needed much persuading. Well, a weak one, a new one, from Earth where they grow them soft, and can afford to. That didn't steam me up anymore: what could I expect from her? But from him . . .

A second went by before either of them saw me, and it was Yonge, the kid, who spotted me first. He froze. He didn't say a thing, or do a thing; he just froze. Panic, of course. He was a kid all right, still a boy and nothing more.

I said, "All right, Christie," and when she heard my voice she turned around and saw me, too. A cool customer, not like the boy; I'll say that much for her. There was strength in that one, if you could get at it.

"No," she said. "I won't."

If you could get at it and make it work for you; she was a good one, a lot of potential once the soft cover had been knocked off. "Of course you won't," I said, without moving. The door shut behind me. "But you're going to."

"She's coming with me," the kid said.

It was a brave speech, and he actually took a step toward me. It was as brave as he was likely to get, but even that much surprised me. Well, he thought he was in love, and it does something for you along those lines, they tell me. Every gaff has its own value. If you can pay the price; but he couldn't. I said, "Don't be ridiculous," thinking that some reminder of the way he looked might be a help. But he didn't step back.

"You can't stop us," he told me. Big heroics, a lot of noise; it meant nothing, but it was troublesome. I looked at Christie instead, and I looked as certain as I felt.

That got to her, of course. "Maybe—" she started to say, suddenly, and then: "Alex, maybe she's—"

I cut in to make it ride my way. "Maybe she's right?" I said. "I'm right; you can believe that. Where do you think you're going to go?"

On edge, as they were, a good, practical question was an upsetting ball to field. I watched them try for it, and Christie came in first, with a voice as uncertain as I'd hoped it would be.

"Alex—"

He looked at her for a second. Then he tried calming her down, which was one of the mistakes I thought he might make. "We can make out," he said. "Don't worry about that; we can make out, all right."

She looked no more convinced, and I drove that nail home: "Not where they can hear my word." Alex looked directly at me for a second, a flash of desperation and something else I couldn't identify. Christie was looking at him, and then at me, moving very slowly and cautiously. "Remember this," I said. "Remember that Christie is a runaway. A scat. Do you think I can let that go?"

He surprised me. He said, "I'll buy her from you. I'll buy her contract."

The idea was even possible, and for some reason I hadn't thought of it; I suppose I could not truly imagine him wanting her that much. Valuing that little scat in terms of true, hard cash . . . well, I heard myself think that, and I said, "What with? You've got nothing."

"My father—" he said, but that was a blind, and I knew it, and didn't bother to let him finish.

"Is a little too busy right now to bother with this." I gave him one more prod. "And you ought to be, too."

Christie had given up looking at him; she knew where the decision waited, and she stared at me with open, waiting eyes. "Alex, please—" she began, without moving her head. But he shook her off with a gesture.

"I tell you, I'll buy—"

It was a farce. "You've got no money and no standing," I told him. "Not yet you haven't. Don't talk for air's sake if you can't back it." I let that sink in for a second, while nobody said anything or, maybe, even moved, and then I added: "Meanwhile, I've got work to do. You're holding me up. Come on, Christie."

He wasn't ready to give in yet, though there was nothing left for him to fight with. He started up again, this time from a different angle. "My father won't let you—"

"Your father's busy," I said, perfectly calmly. "Busy being ill, and busy with Diamond. And what makes you think he'd have sympathy with this careless, silly scat try of yours?"

It rocked him, but not badly enough. "When I control—" he began.

"If you control anything," I said. "There's a fight on—do you remember that?"

Christie saw that the decision had been made, and now, for the first time, I saw the edge of panic bite at her. Her eyes wavered, she turned to him, she began: "Alex, help me—" and I cut in before he could find the words to make his stand last a little longer. I don't like trouble, and I cut it short where I can.

"There's no help for you," I said. "Not that kind of help, and not now. You earn some cash—it isn't hard, maybe a year or so—and then you'll be on your own. Then you can do what you like."

The words forced her to turn back toward me, and to reply to me. She said, "I know. You've told me that." Her voice was the same, absolutely sweet, absolutely calm and distant; it had broken only once, in that stupid call for help. She was a prize, a real find, and she was going to be a star for me.

"And it's true," I told her, and then turned to the kid myself. "Alex, is it true?" I asked him.

He was still off-balance. "It's a year," he said, giving me a truthful answer because it was all he could think of to do. "And probably more than that."

Christie said, without a trace of tremor, "I can't stand it." She said no more than that. It hung in the air for a second and I said, flat and businesslike:

"Sure you can. Give you another week or so of training, and you'll stand it fine." I even gave her part of a grin. I was telling the truth, too: a week was all it would take. Drugs, of course, where needed; they're not expensive, and they do the job. Of course, I'd rather work without them, and keep the overhead down, but in certain cases there's no substitute for that sort of technique. And the expense wouldn't be too bad, over a short period of time: the girl's fees would absorb it easily enough, especially if she turned out as well as I thought she might.

The idea of training reached her, of course, and she choked out one word: "Never—" and stood hopelessly between the two of us. The kid had to say something, and he said it.

"I'll take you away—"

"Where?" I asked him. "Off-planet?"

I had him confused and off-balance, and I'd jabbed at him hard; Christie stood and watched him hopelessly; there was only one thing he could do, and he did it. Without one full second of warning, and with no sound at all but a sort of grunt he probably didn't know he was producing, he rushed me.

I stepped aside, naturally, and he came up to me and past me by an inch. I hit him at the side of the head with my balled fist, only once but just right, and when he went down I had no more trouble with Christie. I hadn't thought there would be.

Of course, I left instructions with the girls there to cart him home, and took Christie into the back rooms by myself. There was a lot of work to be done, and I was beginning to feel crowded: there didn't seem to be a lot of time left to work in.

FIFTEENTH CALL

CHAPTER 29

What is this life? What asken man to have?
Now with his love, now in his colde grave,
Alone, withouten any companie.

—from *The Canterbury Tales,*
by Geoffrey Chaucer

ALEX YONGE

CHAPTER 30

I came awake without knowing exactly where I was, lost in the aches and dreams of all that had happened to me; past and future began to mix themselves in my mind, and I might have been any age, in any condition, lost in the absolute darkness between the worlds: there was no way to tell. Then, very slowly, I opened my eyes and saw light, which hurt the way all knowledge hurts, the way becoming an adult, at last, has to hurt; and my eyes focused and I recognized my own room. The walls were nearly bare and of a distant, meaningless color, and the scattering of toys and films was still there, virtually the same assortment I'd had since my fourth or fifth year. Nothing had changed, in fact; I was home again; and for a second or so I truly wondered if everything I remembered had been a dream. Now, that's the sort of thing you find people in the 3V sells doing, all that sort of dramatic displacement, but it happens in actual life as well—or, at any rate, it happened to me, then and there, as if I'd somehow turned into a 3V character without realizing the fact. Perhaps, I was telling myself, Christie had been a dream, and Diamond, and all of that; perhaps we were back now, simply, to life itself, life on Three, nothing more, and nothing more demanding. For some strange reason, connected perhaps with the continuing ache in my head and the tension in my body, the emotion that came to me was actually, primarily, the emotion of relief.

Outside, daylight shone, and my own mind, the peculiar clock which ticks on no matter what else I do, or refrain from doing, told me that only a few hours had passed; I was living through just the same day on which everything had (perhaps not) happened. But the ache in my head grew, and when I tried to sit up the blood began painfully to pound away inside my skull and my neck, and pain brought its usual certainty: I was not involved in a dream. I lay back, with that thought bright and unclear at the front of my mind, and after a few minutes I tried to sit up again, and this time I was capable of it. Actual life had returned, and in spite of some remaining pain I was ready to deal with it. Outside my room, I began to hear a faint noise, as if someone out there were talking, moving, waiting for me. I shifted on the bed, which creaked once, and as if my own noise had been a signal the door of my room opened, very slowly, with an effect of caution.

I said, "Who is it?" The safeties, I noticed, were off; the door gave no alarm, but only slid silently open. Well, whoever had brought me in hadn't set them, which was natural, and which explained, I thought, the noise outside: he'd stood guard instead of leaving the matter to mechanicals, not knowing in what condition I might awaken. Now, with that explanation, I began to remember everything, and in clarity, and so it was suddenly hard for me to talk or to move; the loss, the loss went through me like a fever, and my body became more tense and more rigid: that action brought a stab of pain back to my neck, but I scarcely noticed it.

A voice said: "Are you—are you all right, Mr. Yonge?" The words were timid, but the voice contained within itself the habit of authority and of sure statement; after less than a second I recognized it.

One of the doctors. I said, "I'm awake. Come in." And I was thinking that she had hit me; she had actually dared to hit me. She had led me on to it, put me in position for that one blow; I could see all of that now, much good it did me. She was a bright woman. And she had Christie. I said, "No," and the doctor, standing in the open doorway, a little man with a firm mouth and wide eyes, took a single step back.

"Mr. Yonge, I—"

"All right," I said, "I didn't mean you. Come in." I gestured at him, but that fright of his remained as he came to my side and stood near the bed, looking down at me. After a second he spoke.

"How do you feel?"

I shrugged: motion was not very painful then. Of course I said nothing about my own troubles to a hired professional, but only: "Well enough."

The fright, strangely, grew; and then there was no strangeness left at all. Everything was explained. "Can you—can you come down the hall?" he asked me quietly, and stepped back without waiting for my answer.

It was happening, at last.

Oh, I'd expected it. For the few seconds it took me to go down the hall to his room, I had even, seriously and thoroughly, thought about it. But, standing there, facing the bed on which he lay, it was all, suddenly, entirely new. I didn't feel anything—not surprise, not terror or sadness, simply nothing at all: it was as if there were no more room in myself for feelings. It was as if I weren't there, as if I were seeing some sort of 3V, some sell or other; no more than that. There wasn't any more; emotion would come later, and nothing I could do might better arrange matters. This was not in my control.

His mouth opened, dry and slow, and a few words filled the air, thinly and distantly. "Alex, I wanted to say something—"

He stopped then. I waited in silence for a little time, and then asked him, "Yes?"

But his mind was elsewhere, battling, judging. At last he said, "It's in your hands now."

"Don't be—" I meant to sound cheerful, to give hope in that dim room, but he cut me off almost with impatience, and his voice grew louder, more assured.

"It's in your hands now," he snapped. "Stop whining at me."

I said, "Yes." No more than that; the word seemed to calm him slightly, but when he continued to speak his voice maintained its old tenor, and its old force.

"And you'll have to be an adult," he said flatly. "Live up to it. Sometimes—I don't know, but sometimes I think—" He paused, and his voice dropped to its original dry whisper. "Alex?"

"Yes?" I said. His eyes stared into the gloom of that place, and he moved a little in the bed.

"Are you still there?" he asked me softly, and then began to add: "It's hard to—"

"I'm still here," I said. Once again there was a silence, and then he spoke again. He did not move now, as if he conserved all his energy for speech; yet his voice was weak. Time was passing, time went sliding on while I stood, and while he spoke there.

"Be an adult," he said, choosing every word, shaping it with difficulty but with a remaining clarity. "Think it through; think everything through. Be careful, be fast, be thorough." He stopped and took two or three deep, shivering breaths of the room's still air.

I said, "Yes," and waited. Time passed, I felt nothing; there seemed to be no sound in that place except for our voices, which died without echo. Yet their echo continued in my mind, and I heard the same words repeat themselves, over and over again, while I stood there and waited.

"I pass it on to you," he said. "These are witnesses, here." That was a formal declaration, and I heard the others murmur, then, with a sense of surprise, being so suddenly surrounded by noise. I could hardly let the declaration pass, but he never allowed me to finish.

"Dad—"

"Don't worry about Diamond," he said suddenly, and almost at his normal speed. "Diamond has no chance."

"All right," I said. His head moved slowly to one side and then to the other; his eyes closed and then, a little at a time, opened again. He breathed, a harsh single sound, and spoke as he seemed to watch me.

"You don't believe that," he said. "I can see it now." He spoke very slowly, his voice faint, his body absolutely still. "Diamond thinks the Reel is for one man," he said. "But the Reel is—" He stopped altogether, then, and when he spoke it was in an entirely new voice, a hollow, assured, distant sound I had never heard before. The curtains of the room shivered and were still. "I see it now," he said. "You understand. I see a great deal now."

Perhaps he was talking to me; I could not tell. I said, "Yes," and he went on without giving any sign that he had heard me. He said a few words, that was all:

"A great deal."

And then he stopped. He did not jerk, or shriek: he only stopped. Muscles in his body tightened and relaxed and the body was through with motion. He had gone.

Then a doctor moved, watched, told me that he was dead; but I didn't need to be told. The room had its own sudden, sharp odor, and seemed to me to sustain an equally sudden sense of chill. I stood, nevertheless, without thinking of what I was doing or what should be done, until one or another of the doctors there led me away and out of that place. As I left it they came to me, the shivering and the fear.

The fear: that was, of course, the worst, and worse because I had no idea of its object: I was simply frightened, terrified even, in darkness. When I thought of Christie, I was sick, physically sick with the force of fear, and so I went to my own room and sat on a chair there, without getting up; I sat there while time passed, time slipped by, quite a length of it moving from darkness to darkness; downstairs, of course, they pushed and milled, shouted and passed, just as usual, since nothing had changed for them; nothing, in truth, had changed.

I wanted to ask him why I was afraid, and he was the only person I could not ask, the only person of whom I could not even think. And then I wanted, simply, to ask him—to ask him anything at all; can you understand that? I wanted to ask him . . . I wanted him.

I sat for a long time there, without moving at all.

SIXTEENTH CALL

CHAPTER 31

Ask not what your country can do for you;
ask what you can do for your country.

—from the Inaugural Address of
President John Fitzgerald Kennedy

CHRISTIE CHESSON

CHAPTER 32

I don't think it's any of my job to talk about these things, and they aren't anything I truly understand in any case; I certainly don't want to repeat them for myself, even by telling them to your recorders; that means I've got to remember what actually did happen, and what it was like, and it's no pleasure for me to do that. You call me a citizen of Earth, of course, but Earth didn't seem to be much help when I needed the help, and calling me a citizen of the Comity, which includes the Reel, or Three, whatever its name is going to be, doesn't improve matters: that's just a form of words. Trade agreements and agreements of independent function and such are words, too, and no more than words until you get caught up by them, until Earth refuses to recognize a distress clause, as it does on the Reel—as you know; I don't have to go into that.

But—I'm just talking to delay matters, I suppose. What you're asking me to do is simply not that big, not that important an action: simply that I tell you what happened. And I imagine I might as well. I could even invent a rationale for myself about it, and tell myself that it would do some good, though I don't truly believe that for an instant.

Maybe (I might say this) it might make someone, somewhere, stop and think for a minute. It might, sometime, in some way, make one customer less for the sort of trade I found myself in. That is, after all, the sort of thing people do say, to justify stories like mine, the sort of thing people have always said; but I no longer understand what difference it would make. There are always more customers. There are always more tourists. If there were one less, or one more, nobody could conceivably notice. There are so many that—that they can all go and hang themselves. I mean that. Quite sincerely, they can all go and take gas and get out of my air.

I used to be a tourist myself, you understand; of course you know that. Truly. But I didn't know any better then, you see, and I was simply out for a good time, a plain, simple, normal good time. I suppose you could call it curiosity, the thing that got me here in the first place, nothing more, or more demanding, than that. I'd never seen the Reel (in those times I thought of it as a place I could see, a sort of display, not truly a world of its own), and when the money arrived—I had an aunt, we'd never been terribly close but there were no other surviving relatives, or none that she knew about, or that I did, and when I got what was left after the Inheritance Gift—and that's the sort of thing my Earth Citizenship did for me, that Inheritance Gift—40 percent was what it came to . . .

You don't want to hear about all that; I'm wasting tape and time. All right.

There was enough, at any rate, to take a trip here, to spend some time and look around, and to return; though of course it wasn't at all that simple. I made my plans, but my plans were an interesting fiction, a story: they had nothing to do with the Reel.

There is always something more here, you see, something around the next corner or inside the next shop, and curiosity finished what curiosity had started, because whatever you want to see or to experience costs money: everything costs money on the Reel. A great deal of what was available here was new to me, and if some of it seemed simply bizarre or dull there was always something else, something of true interest. I don't even know whether I noticed that the money for my return trip was gone.

No, that's a lie: of course I noticed. There are a few worlds in the Comity, or so I've heard, where a visitor posts bond equal to the amount of a return ticket, but the Reel doesn't manage matters that way; later, of course, I found out why it prefers not to. And all the talk about independent function keeps a system like the Reel's operating without trouble or interference, as you know. But you don't know what it means, or I hope you don't: you look like rather normal, rather nice people to me. I wouldn't like to think you know what the Reel's system means.

I needed money, and I had to do something about it quickly, because it was quite too late to think about saving, or about being sensible. There were the gambling palaces, of course, and I thought I might be lucky there—because I *had* to be lucky, you see. For no better reason than that, but it seemed, at the time, enough. Equally of course, I wasn't lucky, and then there was no money at all: there was nothing left, except for the Tourist Office. You will have seen the notices all around, telling you that if you're from off-world and you have any trouble at all you ought to go directly to a Tourist Office, where they'll straighten you out.

They told me, at one of those Offices, what I'd have to do, and I left and went to the Representation of Earth, and spoke to a few secretaries there, though I couldn't get very high into the organization. I suppose I was no more than an average case; I suppose there are a lot like me. It was the Representation who told me all about the various treaties and agreements, and left me with the absolute knowledge that there was nothing to be done. Nothing, at any rate, except what the Tourist Office had suggested.

They told me, you see, that I could earn enough money for a return trip. They told me the work would be light, and that the job wouldn't last over six months local time, which is not too different from the time I've been used to all my life.

All right: there was nothing for me to go back to, but I wanted to go back. The Reel is a vacation resort, and I couldn't imagine living in a vacation resort; by its nature, it's a place you come to, and leave again within a fairly short time. (Of course people do live here, but I couldn't truly imagine that, either, until I had had some experience of them.) I had no man waiting at home, I had no relatives; though I could find a job easily enough when I went back there was no job waiting for me: six months seemed a short enough time. I was, after all, alone in the world; why not take their offer? Especially since there seemed no other answer; if I could not, finally, leave the Reel, I'd have to work there in any case.

Of course, when I met Marge Sunday, and she began to explain the nature of that light, that simple, job to me, I had an answer to that "why not" of mine. But by then, naturally, it made no difference: it was much too late, and what else was there for me to do?

You do see that, don't you? That there was nothing else?

In any case . . . you don't want to hear about the next few days, the next little time, because you've heard that, or so you tell me. I'm sorry. I ramble on here as if neither of us had duties or schedules. I'm sorry. Just give me a second and we'll go right on and finish this up.

I suppose it has to be finished up.

He came, of course: Alex. But he made no difference to anything that happened, you understand; he made a difference only to the way I felt about what happened, and that wasn't important to anyone but me. In that first little time, it was important to me. He made his promises, he began, and then she walked in, and they took him away. I didn't even see that, you know; I was taken away as well, and put back into the training rooms, where I had been and where I had learned. They weren't truly so bad: it was only the way I felt about it. I suppose that's true.

And on the next day, Alex didn't come. I supposed that Marge Sunday had forbidden him in some way, made it too difficult for him, and I tried to imagine how she had done that, but I couldn't picture what would be difficult for Alex. He lived in so different a world, in so different a way. I don't think she would have threatened me, you see, in any way that would have kept me away; but Alex was different, of course. That was just a word, too: "different," but I used it as if it explained a lot of things. And I had no time to worry over him, because I had a customer.

I was ready, you see. I'd been trained: I'd had the books to read, and I'd been shown how my protection operated. There were a good many books, though the books didn't give me any idea of what it would be like; they were only words on paper and some of them didn't even truly disturb me or make me afraid. And there was quite a lot of protection, naturally: Marge Sunday didn't want anyone hurt, because that way the hurt one would lose future commissions: Marge Sunday wanted the money, you see, the way that everyone on the Reel always does want the money.

And then I had watched through one-ways, watched sessions with other girls taking care of other customers: that was bad, because that was no longer a parade of words I could push away, and I'd been sick with what I'd seen. I'd been sick over and over again. And now I was finished with being sick.

I was ready to begin earning money. Money for Marge Sunday, of course, and I suppose money for me as well. The only trouble was that I somehow didn't seem to exist anymore; I didn't seem important; I had no feeling that I cared what happened to me, if you understand what I'm trying to say. There was still a spark, or something like a spark, because I could think of Alex: he had come, and he had offered me a way out, or what might have been a way out. If you belong to the Reel, then that would be the reason for the spark. If you don't, if you're like me and you don't belong, I don't know what reason there might be for that little remaining amount of care and feeling, except simply Alex, simply and only Alex himself, whether a reason like that is right, or wrong, or in fact makes any sort of sense at all. I wouldn't know; I can't tell.

But: he smiled at me, that man, fat and fifty, stern and shaky, a small man with a timid smile that went sharp at the edges with fear or trouble or need, and hands, in spite of his fat, as thin as bundles of sticks, all clasped in rolls of weight at the wrists, his fingers moving slowly in and out of the fists he made. His voice was breathy and distant and very eager: "Are you going to be a good girl?" he asked me. The door was shut, we were all alone.

I whimpered, "Don't hurt me," just the way I'd been taught to do, just the way he wanted me to do, and I could see the very sound of my own voice light candles that flamed up behind his eyes; those eyes widened, and his breath got faster. He tensed for a second and then came up close to me, very close to me and slapped me across the side of my face. My head rocked, as it had been taught to do, though of course I wasn't hurt at all, and my eyes closed and opened again and saw him still standing there.

He said, "You're going to be taught—" in the same distant voice, but his own breath choked him as he watched me and he couldn't say anything more. He hit me, that time, with his fist and I went backward, staggering, of course, and fell on the floor, the padded and plastic floor which looked so hard and cold to him, as it was meant to do.

He came after me, then, and I moaned as I had been taught; my clothing ripped as it was meant to do. I—don't want to talk about it anymore. I'm sorry.

I don't; I can't. It was over, after a time, I don't know how long, and then there was another one, of course.

And after him, another one; I don't know how many there were, and I don't know how long a time went by; I knew they were there when they hurt me, even a little, in spite of all the protection, but when there wasn't any hurt I don't know at all.

I don't know at all.

Please. Stop. Stop this.

That's all.

Stop.

SEVENTEENTH CALL

CHAPTER 33

Make the conquerors running, with their hair and other light things streaming in the wind, and with brows bent down: and they should be thrusting forward opposite limbs; that is, if a man advances the right foot, the left arm should also come forward. If you represent anyone fallen, you should show the mark where he has been dragged through the dust which has become changed to blood-stained mire, and roundabout in the half-liquid earth you should show the marks of the trampling of men and horses who have passed over it.

Make a horse dragging the dead body of his master, and leaving behind him in the dust and mud the track of where the body was dragged along.

Make the beaten and conquered pallid, with brows raised and knit together, and let the skin above the brows be all full of lines of pain; at the sides of the nose show the furrows going in an arch from the nostrils and ending where the eye begins, and show the dilatation of the nostrils which is the cause of these lines; and let the lips be arched displaying the upper row of teeth, and let the teeth be parted after the manner of such as cry in lamentation. Show someone using his hand as a shield for his terrified eyes, turning the palm of it toward the enemy, and having the other resting on the ground to support the weight of his body; let others be crying out with their mouths wide open, and fleeing away. Put all sorts of armor lying between the feet of the combatants, such as broken shields, lances, swords, and other things like these. Make the dead, some half-buried in dust, others with the dust all mingled with the oozing blood and changing into crimson mud; and let the line of the blood be discerned by its color, flowing in a sinuous stream from the corpse to the dust. Show others in the death agony grinding their teeth and rolling their eyes, with clenched fists grinding against their bodies and with legs distorted. Then you might show one, disarmed and struck down by the enemy, turning on him with teeth and nails to take fierce and inhuman vengeance; and let a riderless horse be seen galloping with mane streaming in the wind, charging among the enemy and doing them great mischief with his hoofs.

You may see there one of the combatants, maimed and fallen on the ground, protecting himself with his shield, and the enemy bending down over him and striving to give him the fatal stroke; there might also be seen many men fallen in a heap on top of a dead horse; and you should show some of the victors leaving the combat and retiring apart from the crowd, and with both hands wiping away from eyes and cheeks the thick layer of mud caused by the smarting of their eyes from the dust.

And the squadrons of the reserves should be seen standing full of hope but cautious, with eyebrows raised, and shading their eyes with their hands, peering into the thick, heavy mist in readiness for the commands of their captain; and so, too, the captain with his staff raised, hurrying to the reserves and pointing out to them the quarter of the field where they are needed; and you should show a river, within which horses are galloping, stirring the water all around with a heaving mass of waves and foam and broken water, leaping high into the air and over the legs and bodies of the horses; but see that you make no level spot of ground that is not trampled over with blood.

—from the *Notebooks of Leonardo da Vinci,*
edited by Edward McCurdy

ALEX YONGE

CHAPTER 34

There was a doctor standing next to me then, a face that seemed strange enough to me, though I had the shadow of impression that I had seen it before, casting a shadow on my seated self, leaning down and asking me in a voice that seemed quite distant whether I were willing. I stood up, it seemed to me very quickly, but still he had time to move out of my way and stand respectfully apart, waiting; I suppose I was angry.

"I'm not willing," I said, and my own voice sounded, in my ears, as distant as his had seemed. "I don't want a shot; I want nothing at all now. I don't want to be calmed down." It surprised me, a little, that I could mouth such sounds and he take them and pretend somehow to understand them; but all this feeling of strangeness began quickly enough to pass as the anger burned it away.

Strangeness was not all that passed. He began: "But—"

"Just get out," I said, already beginning to realize my position, and the weight of it, and its responsibility. "Leave me alone."

"But if you'll only listen—"

"Listen?"

And I did, then, and heard it: the sound downstairs, the sound which had already changed, and was becoming every second something new, and something more threatening. Yet my first thought was slow, and timid.

I said only, "A fight."

"Not between the tourists," the doctor told me heavily, and watched me as I moved to the door, and stopped there without opening it, hearing the noise grow in volume and change again in pitch.

"Then—" I said, inescapably, automatically, that word, but it was hardly needed, and I said no more: I knew. Anger had dissolved the strangeness, and now all my father, too, was to go to the furnace in his turn; there was no time left for him, no time at all. I had not even time to mourn, hardly time to realize what had become of my dutiful stasis and my own surprise of feeling.

Diamond was there, Diamond himself perhaps, downstairs, in the Yonge Palace: the fight had begun.

I was down and on the last flight of stairs that led into the main room, the Palace stairs, slick and showy, steps ahead of the doctor, who pattered after me as if he could do some action to soften the responsibility he was feeling. The scene below made no sense at all to me, at first, refused to fall into a pattern, but then the pattern came, as I knew it would: people milled, shouted, struck, and I could see Diamond's men fanning out from the arched inner entrance and taking over the games, simply crushing their way into power by weight of numbers and letting the games run on for the few who wanted more play. The tourists were in groups of a few each, scattered round the edge of the main rooms; naturally enough, they wanted no part of this action, and a lot of them would have left. Those would not be back, but would find other palaces to work off their drives on: that, of course, hardly mattered to any of us, since fresh shiploads kept on coming, new ones who wouldn't have the word about our fight, or would have the word in such a way that the place looked even more "romantic" to them.

I didn't know whether Diamond had been tipped to my father's blanking out, but he'd have known of the injury, and picked the right time for his move.

I shouted from the head of the last flight there, stopping my glide for a second and standing to watch and wait. Heads turned to look at me and then went back to the fight. A group of bodyguards started up toward me and I tripped the glide again and went down to meet them. I think, even then, I knew what I had to do.

I headed for the arches at the front, but I had to pass by one roulette setup, its board half smashed and men on both sides battling still. The bodyguards crushed two out of my way, and I heard their screams as they went down; I recognized neither. Most of Diamond's men were strangers, probably from other cities; Diamond himself wasn't there, as I'd seen from stairtop. I would have recognized a single directing leader, and there was no sign of that. Somewhere a mechanism broke down and began to whine, reaching a higher and higher peak of shattering sound. Over it, men shouted; my own men, outnumbered, fought and went down.

Of course a group of Diamond's hirelings came for me directly: lop off the head and our Palace has no further existence; what difference does it make to a stickman which of us he works for, though he has to show loyalty?

But the guards stuck with me, good professionals doing a professional job, and I had only a little to do myself. More of the tourists were leaving; the mechanism went on whining and the shouting grew. Somebody's hand swung at me and I chopped at it with the side of my palm and sent it down and away. A bodyguard grunted and disappeared, leaving a hole in the air, but I grabbed the gun he tossed, in reflex, as he dropped, and used it, fanning out a wide beam without caring much who I hit. It quieted things down, and either I melted out the mechanism or somebody else chopped it out: the whine stopped. Screams seemed to leap nearer in the air.

I'd given my directions to the guards, and we got through. Through the arches and out of the Palace, into the open air.

Diamond's men had the place, and Diamond's men controlled it, which didn't matter at all. He had to be beaten, and beaten thoroughly, before we signed on to spend the rest of our lives warring with him, destroying tourist revenue in nothing but a battle for control; the man had neither sense nor brains. And there was more I wanted for myself (being still childish when I might afford it), and gratitude would help me buy it out.

Everything was very simple, of course; but there wasn't much time. There wasn't much time at all.

EIGHTEENTH CALL

CHAPTER 35

What do I fear? myself? there's none else by:
Richard loves Richard; that is, I am I.
Is there a murderer here? No. Yes, I am:
Then fly. What, from myself? Great reason why:
Lest I revenge. What, myself upon myself?
Alack, I love myself. Wherefore? for any good
That I myself have done unto myself?
O, no! Alas, I rather hate myself
For hateful deeds committed by myself!
I am a villain: yet I lie, I am not.
Fool, of thyself speak well: fool, do not flatter.

—from *Richard III,* Act V, Scene iii,
by William Shakespeare

MARGARET SUNDAY

CHAPTER 36

They were just too many for us: that's all there was to it, in the end. If you would rather have a complicated explanation of exactly what happened, step by step and inch by inch, you're not about to get one from me; I'm sorry, but it's not what I remember. It all seemed very simple, right up to the end, and the details weren't worth keeping in my mind. All right?

I'd gone back to the Flag House that next day, to check back on Christie. When you get a loose couple of minutes like the one she'd had, with that "rescue" or whatever the Yonge kid wanted to call it, things can work out badly for you, and I wanted to be sure Christie was in trim and knew which side was up, and so on. I didn't want her out of line for a day or even more than that, and nothing succeeds like a personal check-out. Then I know it's being done right.

I was in the Flag House when they hit.

I suppose—I must have thought even at the time, without piecing together the reports I got later, and elsewhere—I suppose they hit several places at once. They certainly seemed to be enough men for the job: there were enough, or there seemed to be enough, to take over the city by sheer force of numbers. Though of course only one of those men counted; he was there, too. Standing right there, Diamond himself, overseeing things and even in the thick of the fight here and there.

Naturally, we'd got the customers out the back jumps first thing, before they knew anything was wrong. In a place like that, an attack was all they'd have needed for a true and final panic, the thing itself; enough of what boiled up inside them was waiting for that sort of ending, anyhow. There were a few guards around and they made a stand, and some of the girls made a stand of their own, but all that sort of thing didn't even look convincing: we just didn't have the weight, and we knew it. I was with the girls in a central room wondering which way to jump, before very long; the exits weren't for us, since they'd be mined or manned by the time we got to thinking we'd truly need them.

That door was metal, and metal in lock, not easy to open and not simple to figure, but it didn't matter at all; Diamond didn't bother with unpinning it. He beamed his way through instead; the door melted out; and he stepped through the opening and looked at us, that slim, distant little man, and Christie screamed. Of course it would be Christie. Nobody else made a sound for what must have been ten seconds. Behind Diamond, in the outer rooms, there were a few noises, but nothing important, nothing that meant anything: just the background crash and stamp of takeover. Just the end.

Diamond said, "It's all over." His voice was as distant as the rest of him, an icy sound under tight rein. He'd crack open if I found the entry for a wedge; there were no halfways for that one. But I had no time for a wedge, or for anything else.

I said, reflexively, "Get out of here." He didn't seem to mind that; he didn't even smile, or show he'd heard me.

"It's over," he said again. "I've got men outside—"

I cut him off there, prying for a last advantage. "I know that," I told him, as tight and hard as I could make myself sound. "We stood them off—"

"Until you were beaten," he said, just as calmly as before. He looked around at us, the eight or nine girls standing frozen, the tight central room itself; then he came back to me where I'd put myself, nearest to him, at the head. Where I had to be, of course, if we were to have any chance at all. "Well, you're beaten," he told me. "You're over. And I'm here to give you a choice."

I looked round, too, for the effect, but it didn't put him off-balance any that I could see. "Do you think you can hold this place?" I asked him.

He answered me just as if he were interested in the talk; behind me, I heard one of the girls catch her breath and whimper. That sound went on, and after a second I knew it belonged to Christie. "I think I can hold it," he said. "I've got other men, elsewhere. I think I can hold the city."

The words came out of me in a sort of astonishment; we'd known, we'd all known, from the beginning, what he had been aiming for, but the statement of it was still a shock. We lived independent of each other, leasing and trading as we found it helpful; the idea of a city under a single control was new, and threatening. "The city—"

"It's mine," he said flatly. "The Reel's going to be mine as well: this is the first step." He didn't waste a word or a second on it, as if he had thought out all the talk long before; he stopped and waited for me to take my place in it.

I said, "They won't let you—"

"Who?" he asked me sharply enough. "Other cities? Why should they care?"

And he was right, of course. Christie went on whimpering, as if she wanted to say something but hadn't the words or the breath for the job. There was no time to shut her up; time had run out. I said, at last, "What's your choice?"

"Oh," he said, as if I'd had to remind him of it. His eyes roved and came back to me, not as if they enjoyed what they saw; he was recording it, no more. He seemed to be running through, simply, a dull part in a dull play. "That," he said. "I could have had you killed—I've done it with others. Small-timers. But you're different, you and Yonge and the others, the top operators. I want you to run things—for me. I want it done that way, you see."

I heard him out and then had to put what he'd said back into language I could understand. At last I asked him, "Take your orders?"

"However you want to look at it."

I was still jockeying for position, for a second's time, a chance to find the opening, a final grab at winning, without knowing why. I said, "And if we refuse?"

"I don't have to spell it out for you, Marge."

He called me by name, then and there, for the first and last time, and I felt a flash of anger like veritable heat, but there was no room in that situation for anger to control me; I put it down, refusing the indulgence of that feeling, and strained for thought. But all my thought had one end;

there was no room at all, there was no time at all: I had run out of moves, and the game was over.

Christie said, then, very suddenly, "Yes," and his eyes went to her; mine did as well, but she never looked at me.

Her eyes were wide and blank. Diamond said, "What?"

"I'll be—" she began, and stopped, and seemed to think, though her expression somehow never changed. Then she went on, more slowly, as if she had to hear her own words to know what she thought at all. "It doesn't make any difference, does it? You, or her. I'll work the same, just the same." Each sentence came out entire, and she stopped, and then the next group of words was made. She stared at Diamond as if she was seeing nothing at all. "I'll do the same things. Only—" She paused there for a second, but nobody else moved, and nobody spoke. "Keep me here," she said, and her voice had more urgency in it; her eyes blinked, once, and blanked once more. "Let me stay here. Don't let me go outside."

She was finished, then, for a second, and Diamond pulled himself away and turned to me, and said, "What's this?"

"Forget her," I said. "She's not important." There had to be a way for me to turn Christie to my advantage, whatever snap she'd had, whatever had unwound; but there was none. I tried to think again.

"Just keep me here," she told Diamond.

He smiled then, the first and only time, and looked at her, and then, with the insolence that had called me by name, he looked at me. "Is your answer the same?"

"My answer—"

I hesitated, trying to turn him off-balance, trying for anything, or nothing at all, and he took a step forward. The girls remained frozen, all of them staring at that slim little man; he moved an arm jerkily, like a puppet or a man sunk under the needle, and said in a voice almost without breath, "Come on."

"You've won, then," I said, watching him move, but the moment passed and he was himself again: his arm relaxed and he spoke distantly, with assurance, as if once again he had found the right words, the right script for this point in the play.

"I've won."

He had that: he had his moment, in silence, before we heard the new sound, and slowly turned to the melted, ragged door; that was the sound of battle, that was a new fight, and Diamond's second was gone. He started for the door, but he was much too late.

I heard the voice of Alex Yonge, somewhere outside. "Too late for you —" There was more noise.

I don't have to tell you what happened then. It was like a show, like some script out of a workout set, where the customer always wins and the finish upswings faster than any true world: the Marines had arrived; will that give you the idea?

NINETEENTH CALL

CHAPTER 37

If the expectation of hell hereafter can keep me from evildoing, surely *a fortiori* the certainty of hell now will do so?

—from a letter to Charles Kingsley
by T. H. Huxley

WYSS DIAMOND

CHAPTER 38

(The following material has been transcribed from a sound recording made at the Special House #3, otherwise a Flag House, of Margaret Sunday, citizen, and its authenticity is guaranteed by controlled editing staff; by special order.)

If you're all going to watch me you had better hear something, let me tell you that. This is not for your amusement, this is not for you to have fun, not at all, this is what she's doing, that's all—they've got me tied this way, I can't move, all I can do is talk, and you'd better listen, let me tell you that. This is not for you to laugh and watch me when the needle goes in and the end comes down, that doesn't matter at all—you think so, to a man like me? But when the end comes—she could have done this a thousand times, a thousand ways, but this is the one she picked, and you had better listen, there isn't much time; there is not much time. Let me.

No excitement, I can tell you that, there's nothing at all, in fact, watching a man die: men die and that's all, there's the end of it, nothing for you to see and nothing for you to watch, so go; so go and go home, forget it, take your eyes off me and go home; there is nothing here, I'm not the man, this is what she worked up, when the needle comes out and the needle goes home, you can all go away: now. No: I mean that. Now.

I could—this is so new, I had you all, I understood, as long as I could keep forgetting, keep forgotten, all of you are nothing at all when I forget, but this is—I could never describe to her the way I loved her; there was no way for me to do that, you see; there were no words for that. Of course, it's possible, it's always possible—now, you see, now I can't forget anymore, now it's too late for all that—it's possible that I never loved her at all; anything is possible, and that would explain the difficulty; but she was there, you see, she was always there, and she told me only the truth is important, now you remember that, only what you do is important, it doesn't matter what you say, you can boast forever and it means nothing, you're going to be better than the others, not in talk, you remember that, talk's cheap, talk means nothing at all; I had to prove it, and so I had to describe it to her, proving it would do that for me; I don't understand, you see. Of course she is dead now, and she told me the words were nothing; she named me after some other person, long ago, in history, and that was all I ever knew, because she told me find out the rest for yourself, boy, then you'll remember, all right, and first I had to prove to her, I had to prove—what am I saying? You're here now, you're listening to me, you know—go, now, forget it, this is nothing—what am I telling you?

They say a man here takes after his father, you know; they really do say that, but it means nothing; what can it mean to me, ask yourself that? The way I am here. Oh, he was gone, he was dead, they told me about that, you see, and I can't even remember. Take your eyes off me, take away. Like a drowning man, you see, everything is here, it's all in front of me, the way he was; I don't remember any of that, but I had to prove it to her. What she said, you remember that, boy: talk is cheap, and talk is . . .

All right. Now you're going to watch, because you've paid: have you understood that? Any of it? Everybody here pays, all the time, for everything, everybody pays; she might have done this a thousand ways, a thousand times, but this way you all pay, this way you all give it to her, what she wants, the way I wanted; on the Reel, you always pay, that's what we know, is that right? And you pay to watch me, or I pay to watch you; now, what's the difference there, what does it mean? Because it's over, there isn't any proof, not anymore. Not anymore.

When you're gone, that's an end, you see. I want you all to hear this, I can't move here, not at all, and when they come from behind, that boy, I never expected it, and my men don't care, they're working, they don't care who they work for. When you're gone that's an end: correct. You're nothing, you're all nothing up there with your money and your eyes that stay and stay until the needle, which is not at all; this is not going to happen. This is not going to happen. Go. Get out. I can't move here, but I can see her, coming in now, coming and walking toward me and she can't stop me, nobody can stop me, this is not going to happen, you see. It is all very reasonable, when you can pay and when you own it all and when you can pay and prove to her, finally, you had better listen to me, you want to hear me, you don't want this to end and it is not going to end because I have to prove it; at last; yes.

This is not going to happen.

Mother.

TWENTIETH CALL

CHAPTER 39

"Months and years!" my brother would exclaim. "One day is enough for a man to know all happiness. My dear ones, why do we quarrel, try to outshine each other and keep grudges against each other? Let's go straight into the garden, walk and play there, love, appreciate each other and glorify life."

"Your son cannot last long," the doctor told my mother, as she accompanied him to the door. "The disease is affecting his brain."

—from *The Brothers Karamazov*
by Feodor Dostoevski

ALEX YONGE
CHRISTIE CHESSON

CHAPTER 40

Go ahead and say something. I wanted you to end this, I wanted you to have the last word.

There's nothing to say. I didn't do anything. There's nothing for me to tell anybody. Please, you tell what happened; they want to know, it can all be finished now in a few minutes.

When I—are you sure?—when I came in with the men behind me, I had surprise in my favor, and it was all very simple: there was nothing to that. And so of course Marge owed me a return; it was the least she could manage, and she knew the return I wanted, and Christie was released. We were actually married, of course, because Christie wanted it that way—

I didn't care; I don't care.

It's the way things are done on Earth; of course you wanted it that way. You said so; you just don't remember that. And of course the story got around, and the Yonge Palace is doing well out of it. Marge, too, I
1 suppose.

Everything is very profitable.

Certainly; and we're happy. We got what we wanted; it's like a show, it truly is.

We're very happy. Just like a show.

Certainly. Is that all right? Did you want to say something else? Did you want to add anything? Don't be afraid.

I'm not afraid. There's nothing to add.

We're doing fine. You can assure your people—whoever it is wanted this report—that we're doing fine, there's no trouble to speak of anymore: we're showing a profit. Everything's back to normal here; or better than normal. Christie?

I'm all right. I'm fine.
Everything is showing a profit.

LAURENCE M. JANIFER is a well-known writer of science fiction. His many novels include *Knave in Hand, Survivor, Power, A Piece of Martin Cann* and *You Sane Men (Bloodworld).* He lives in New York City.